CW01653859

D. R. CLARK

THE FIFTH FLOOR

First edition

This book was professionally typeset on Reedsy.
Find out more at reedsy.com

Contents

Chapter 1

The overly crowded bus took a turn and proceeded down a busy street filled with cars of people, fighting their way through traffic during rush hour. Emily Frewen hadn't long finished work, she was scrolling on her mobile phone, searching for a place to rent. She had her music cranked up loud, as her earphones blasted rock metal. She'd placed them into her ears ten minutes ago, when the drunken man took the last available seat next to her and began slurring nonsense in her direction.

With her nose picking up a foul smell, she turned and glanced at the man, who now had his head lowered as he slept, drool dripping from his mouth onto his chest. Emily shook her head and peered out of the window. The bus was passing *The Little Green Café*, a rustic vegan place, so she knew she still had another twenty minutes to go until she would have to wake the sleeping drunk and make her way to the exit.

She went back to searching the online property boards, sorting the listings from lowest to highest in price range. When the search results would show the properties she'd already seen that week, she would then broaden the distance a few miles, and contemplate moving to an area she wasn't very fond of or familiar with.

She was desperate to leave her parents' spare room, even if living with parents had its benefits. Emily's mother would wash her clothes and every weekend without fail, she knew to expect a full fry up breakfast cooked by her father. After the breakup with Josh, her ex-boyfriend, moving back home was only supposed to be temporary, nothing more than a month at the most. That was over a year ago now, and even though her parents were great people, Emily missed having a place she could call her own. Somewhere she could play her music as loud as she wanted, choose what to watch on the big TV in the living room, have friends over for food and drinks, and potentially, bring a man back she met on a night out. Whatever the reason, the time had come for her to move out and restart her life again.

Emily wanted to prove to herself - and to Josh - that she was strong, independent and could cope on her own.

Sorting the listings from lowest to highest didn't offer many places Emily would feel comfortable living at. That was, unless she was prepared to give away most of her belongings and move into an apartment the same size as her parents' kitchen!

Rent prices in London are ridiculously high.

Emily ran a finger up her phone screen, bypassing all the properties she'd already seen, and frowned. She stopped when a car beeped at the side of her, gaining her attention. Looking out the window, she saw an angry cyclist give the driver of the car a finger, she chuckled and looked away, catching sight of a faded sign that read *Hollow Street Tyres.* Emily had never paid much attention to the dilapidated building on her commute home before, but now she saw the tyre repair garage was boarded up, and looked as though it had been for some time. There was temporary metal fencing around the perimeter, and the walls of the building slanted to one side, with the roof completely caved in. Emily brought her attention back to her phone screen and came across a posting she hadn't yet seen.

ONE BED APARTMENT AT HOLLOW TOWER.

She looked back out of the window as the bus was passing another building on the corner called *The Hollow Pub and Grill.*

'Weird!' she mumbled, clicked on the posting and read the details.

This stunning one bed apartment offers magnificent views over the idyllic Hollow Park. It has a spacious living room, a fully furnished kitchen and a modern bathroom. The living room has access to an outdoor balcony area that faces east and is designed to seat two people comfortably.

Emily inspected every image closely, zooming in and admiring the kitchen worktops, the tiles on the bathroom floor, the built-in wardrobes in the bedroom and the arched windows. It was perfect, decorated as if she'd chosen the fixtures herself. Even though she was sure a property like this would be way out of her price range, she continued to look anyway, imagining what area of the room she'd have her new *huge* TV, the colour theme for the kitchen and where her bed would fit in the bedroom. In Emily's mind, she was already moved in and living there.

After spending a while visualizing herself in a home that she assumed she couldn't afford, she finally scrolled to the bottom of the page to find the rent price and prepared herself for a shock. She moved the phone closer to her face, unable to believe the figure she was seeing.

That's a typo, she thought. *No way would this be correct!*

The drunk man sitting next to her stood and stumbled away, bringing Emily to lift her head to see the bus had come to a halt next to a row of shops that she wasn't familiar with, and that's when she knew she'd missed her stop.

'Shit!' she hissed, stood and ran to the front before the driver could take off again. 'Wait... wait for me, please!'

Exiting the bus, Emily tapped the call button and listened as it rang. When the machine picked up, Emily hung up and saved the details to her contacts list. She'd give the estate agents a call in the morning, praying that the asking price wasn't a typo, or that somebody else hadn't already gotten there before her and snatched up the property.

She crossed the road and waited at the bus stop on the opposite side.

'Hollow Tower,' she whispered, smiling to herself. 'I like that name.'

Chapter 2

That morning, Emily had waited until nine a.m. to call the office to inquire about the property. She assumed the number belonged to an estate agents, but it was the building owner who had answered her call. The man she spoke with had a wheezy chest and sounded moody, if not a little rude. He was incredibly short with his answers and, going off the chewing and swallowing she heard throughout their conversation, it sounded as if Emily had interrupted him during breakfast.

He had confirmed the rent price listed on the ad was correct and he agreed to meet her at five-thirty p.m. for a viewing.

'Are you excited?' Chloe, Emily's colleague, asked as she found Emily sitting in the canteen with her phone in hand, working through the images of the vacant apartment again.

Emily nodded. 'God, yes! I know I already told you this morning, but I can't even explain how bad I want this place, Chloe. Just take a look.' She turned her mobile around and flicked through the images one by one. 'I can't believe what they're asking for it. It's almost too good to be true, like I'm going to turn up and meet another fifty people waiting to view it. Then learn a bunch of kids have scammed us as they record, laugh and point.'

'You're so paranoid, Emily!' Chloe laughed as she took a seat at the small table and opened her lunch bag, taking out her chicken salad.

'Yeah, I've been told that before.'

'But hey, maybe it isn't a scam. Maybe you just got lucky and found a hidden gem... You deserve some luck, after the dry spell you've had this year. Can you imagine all the sex you can have with all those new guys now?'

'Chloe!' Emily gasped, blushing. 'Is that all you ever think about?'

Chloe took a moment to answer, then bit her lip and nodded. 'Yep, I guess it is.'

'Well, I don't. It's not about sex with strangers for me. It's about having my own space, being able to leave the kitchen in a mess and deal with the pile of dishes later... or the next day, or never! I want to have my alone time after spending all day in this place, listening to complaining customers, you know?'

'Oh, I agree with you about the customers,' Chloe laughed. 'You should have kept the flat last year. I'm telling you; you should have kicked that dick out. Josh was the one who cheated, not you, so he should have been the one to find someplace else to live.'

Last year, when Emily was away on a hen weekend for one of her cousins, the trip had ended a day shorter than planned due to transport problems. She hadn't mentioned it to Josh, instead she grabbed a pizza and a bottle of wine on her way home and planned to surprise him. Only it was Emily who got the surprise after sneaking into the apartment and catching Josh in their bed with another woman.

'What and be reminded every day of Josh and the slut he was in bed with?' asked Emily.

'You're right!'

'That apartment we shared had too many memories, and I wanted to be done with the place. Leave it behind and not have Josh know where I live. Make a fresh start.'

'I understand. Wait, don't tell me he's *still* trying to win you back?' asked Chloe before shuffling some lettuce leaves into her mouth.

Emily nodded and sighed. 'He can't message me anymore because I got a new number, so now he's creating different social media accounts and sending me messages on there, apologising and saying losing me has been his greatest mistake. Honestly, I might delete all my accounts. That way, he can't get to me.'

'Jeez, what a creep!'

'Yep,' Emily agreed. 'He's always been weird; I should have spotted it sooner, when we first started dating.'

'Anyway, enough ex-boyfriend talk,' Chloe said, tapping the table. 'What time is your viewing this evening?'

'Half five,' Emily smiled and went back to looking at the images of the living room. 'I couldn't sleep last night. I know that sounds silly, but out of the all the places I've found and viewed in the last couple of months, I have never wanted one as much as this. It just... *speaks* to me.'

Chloe raised her eyebrow and continued chewing.

'I know, I agree that sounds strange, but it's as if I already live there. Like it's the home I was meant to find.'

'*Okay...*' Chloe chuckled, rolled her eyes, and shot Emily a look as though she sounded crazy.

'The building itself looks beautiful, with arched windows and high ceilings. Most of the apartments have balconies attached. I honestly can't believe it hasn't-'

'Let's hope there hasn't been a mass murder years ago!' Chloe joked and took a sip from her water bottle. When she looked back to Emily, she saw her friend staring at her with a stern look and an expression that said *Seriously?*

She quickly apologised.

The clock in the canteen ticked by, showing Emily it was the end of her lunch break. She stood and waved goodbye to Chloe before heading back to her desk.

After missing her stop, Emily got home a little later than usual last night. She decided not to bring Hollow Tower up to her parents, as she didn't want to disappoint them if she'd found something off about the place and decided to not go any further with the lease. Even though her parents had said they were happy for her to stay if she needed to, Emily still got the feeling they wanted their spare room back. It was originally her mother's sewing area and the place they stored the treadmill and other bits.

Returning to her desk and ready to take a call from another unhappy insurance customer, Emily checked the time on the computer screen. She really couldn't wait to finish and view her potential new home.

* * *

Emily caught the same bus as she would when heading home to her parents and stepped off outside The Hollow Pub and Grill. It looked to be a popular place as the car park had no free parking spaces left. Peering through the windows, she could see tables of people enjoying food in the crowded restaurant area. If it all goes well with the apartment viewing, she imagined stopping here herself one evening, treating her parents to dinner as a thank you for allowing her to move in and for all their help after splitting with Josh the dick.

Hollow Tower was a short walk away, which she reached by crossing through the serene park that faced the old building. Standing at the entrance, Emily inspected decades of charm. The double doors at the front had *HOLLOW TOWER* carved into the brickwork above. She tilted back her head and inspected the many windows, almost all of which emanated a warm, golden glow from the residents' lamps.

That was except for the fifth floor, which stood in complete darkness.

Emily thought nothing of it. She quickly rushed up the path and pressed the buzzer for flat number 2, as instructed by the landlord on their phone call earlier.

The dialling noise was loud and uncomfortable on her ears. A minute later, it stopped as the receiver was picked up. 'Yeah?' a hoarse sounding man grumbled and then coughed.

'Hi, this is Emily... Emily Frewen. I called up earlier about a viewing-'

The door buzzed, and the intercom made a crackling noise before it fell silent, showing the landlord had hung up on his end. Wasting no time, she pushed on the heavy door and stepped inside, immediately inspecting the hallway. To her left and secured to the wall, were over fifteen mailboxes with a small sticker placed on the front of each one and the apartment number written in Sharpie. Just past these was a narrow staircase. A floral print carpet was laid with the pattern almost completely faded in the middle from years of foot traffic. Emily guessed it was fitted when the building was first built.

To her right were two doors, one was flat 1 and the other flat 2. The door further down, flat 2, opened and a chubby man stepped out into the corridor. He was wearing frayed jeans and battered boots, a pale blue shirt tucked scruffily into his jeans with a brown cardigan fully buttoned up. As he stepped closer, Emily noticed he had a tired look about him. His face sagged, and he had greying hair, the whites of his eyes had a faint yellow to them as the skin underneath drooped.

'Emily, I'm-' was all the man said before bursting into a coughing fit, covering his mouth with a hand. He wheezed and cackled before starting again. 'Sorry, I'm Harry Bradshaw. It was me you spoke with earlier.'

'Hi, Harry, thank you for making the time to see me,' said Emily as she went to hold out her hand to shake the landlord's, but then stopped herself and fixed her hair instead. After seeing him splutter his guts up into the palm of his hand, she decided against shaking it.

'Yeah, it isn't a problem,' Harry said in a tone that sounded as if it *was* very much a problem. 'People work all sorts of shifts these days, don't they? I'm forced to make time when I can.'

Emily only smiled back.

'This way, Emily...' Harry pointed and led her over towards the lift along the back wall.

On their way past Harry's apartment, Emily couldn't help but divert her eyes and peek a look in through the open door. Lights danced from a TV, creating shadows on the wall. Emily almost screamed at the sight of an old lady half hidden behind the door. Her eyes were wide and grey, refusing to blink as she kept them focused on Emily as she passed. She was holding a Magna Doodle, the toy famous with children for its ability to draw what they liked and then erase with a simple slide of the magnet on the bottom. Emily slowed her step but didn't stop.

Harry pressed the button for the lift and the doors rattled open, revealing a dimly lit and snug space with a grimy mirror. They both stepped in, and the lift shifted a little.

This is where I die, Emily thought. *I knew the apartment was too good to be true!*

'Don't worry about the movement,' Harry huffed after witnessing Emily's body turn rigid. 'This thing has never once let me down. So, it's the fourth-floor apartment you're here to view.' He pressed the button with the gold number 4 on and Emily noticed the button above was missing. It was nothing but an empty square, the wires behind it exposed.

Emily was readying to ask what was going on with the top floor, why it was in full darkness and why the button to access it was missing. But as she went to open her mouth, the mechanism of the lift began and the compact metal box shrieked and jolted, causing Emily to lean a hand against the murky mirror. 'Jesus! Is this normal?'

'I told you, don't worry about it.' Harry smirked.

With the gears of the lift sounding as wheezy as Harry's chest, they eventually reached the fourth floor and the doors slowly rattled open.

There were four doors in total on this floor, two to her left and two to her right. Flats 11 and 12 were both next to one another on the same wall. Flat 13 shared the wall with a door that had a sign on reading *STAIRCASE*.

'It's the end one,' Harry grunted and led the way. Emily quickly followed behind.

He inserted the key, pushed the door open, and stepped aside for Emily to walk in first. She couldn't help but release a sigh of relief. Since meeting Harry and seeing the carpet on the stairs that needed to be pulled up and burned, then traveling in the rickety lift, she was expecting the apartment to have been a lie. That perhaps the images on the website belonged to another building, one that would be asking for double the rent price. But no, the images weren't lying at all. It didn't matter what state the carpets were in, or that the lift made a worrying noise when in transit, because she wouldn't be spending any time in the hallway, and she'd probably take the stairs rather than the lift to reach her daily step count. So, those were little things she needn't worry about because the apartment looked clean; it had a fresh smell escaping from it and from what she could see, it was just as spacious as the images had made out. No crafty estate agent photography tricks here.

"Let's hope there hasn't been a mass murder years ago!"

Damn it, Chloe! Emily thought, remembering her colleague's words.

'I know what you're thinking...' Harry smirked.

Emily looked at him. 'You do?'

'Yes, and yes, that is a real wooden floor. It isn't that vinyl stuff.' Harry confirmed with a confident smile.

'It's... lovely,' Emily nodded. 'Can I ask what happened to the last resident?'

'Miss Gibson, she moved in with her daughter in Manchester. Had arthritis for years. Things started getting too much for her living alone.'

'Oh, good,' Emily sighed and relaxed a little.

'Good?' Harry asked.

'Not good, just... well... I wanted to know if... if the last person may have died here.'

'Nope,' Harry nodded. 'Nobody has ever died in this apartment. Miss Gibson lived here for the best part of thirty years. It was only last year she paid a handy man to redecorate the place.' Harry pointed to the floor and walls. 'As you can see, it cost her a fair bit.'

They stepped into the kitchen. 'The fridge and washing machine are included in the price. Miss Gibson told me to leave them here, that she wouldn't be needing them. If you want them removed, just say.' Harry said and pulled his mobile from his pocket as a beep, beep, beeping noise sounded. He began typing on his mobile, replying to the message he just received. With the landlord distracted, Emily walked on, inspecting the small window next to the sink and looking out. The view caught the beginning of the park gate, and the busy street to the side of it.

'EMILY!' a voice screamed, and Emily shrieked. She spun on the spot and stared at the landlord. 'What?'

Harry looked up from his mobile and furrowed his brow. 'Excuse me?'

She swallowed, her heart beating rapidly from the sudden shock. 'You... you just called my name.'

Harry looked at her, licked his lips, and shook his head. 'No, sorry. It must have been a car backfiring or something.'

'A car backfiring?' Emily asked.

Harry went to say something else but was interrupted by another voice calling his name.

'Harry, you in here?' a man stepped into the kitchen. 'Sorry, I didn't know you had company.'

He shot Emily a smile and kept his eyes locked on hers for a second longer.

'This is Emily, your *potential* new neighbour,' Harry said, coughed and wheezed into the palm of his hand.

'Nice to meet you,' the man smiled, his eyes darting around

Emily's face. 'I'm Peter Dunn. I live in the apartment next door.'

Emily waved and watched Peter as he brought his attention back to Harry, asking him about a problem with his bathroom plumbing. The neighbour was tall, looming over Harry by a good foot. He looked to be in his thirties, roughly the same age as Emily, and had short, brown hair, a strong stubbly chin and wide shoulders.

'Emily?' Harry said, pulling her out of her stare. 'Why don't you look around the place while I chat with Peter?'

'Sure,' Emily replied and headed for the living room.

'It was nice meeting you, Emily.' Peter called.

'You too, Peter,' Emily said back and left the kitchen. She popped her head into the bathroom and quickly glanced at the bath and shower combination. In the bedroom, she opened and closed the doors of the built-in wardrobes, which proved to be incredibly spacious.

A smile crept onto her face as she pictured her own clothes hanging from the rail. She made her way into the living room. The window faced east, like the ad had promised, and Emily could see out onto the balcony. The ad also said it would seat two people comfortably, which she thought may have been a lie. It was just wide enough for a single chair. Though if that was all they'd been dishonest about in their ad, she really couldn't complain.

The view over the park was soothing and instantly filled her with excitement. Picturing herself sitting outside during the summer evenings while drinking a glass of wine after a hard day's work seemed like a dream. It beats sitting up in her parents' spare room and listening to them argue about what they're watching on TV.

'So, what do you think of the place?' Harry asked, making his way into the living room.

Emily nodded but took a moment to answer, as though she were mulling the question over. Though she already knew the answer—that she absolutely loved the place.

She'd made up her mind and knew she wanted the apartment once Harry first opened the door, and it was clear she wasn't a victim of a scam.

'I think I'd like to take it, Harry,' Emily replied, fighting back the urge to smile from ear to ear.

'Great, I'll go fetch the paperwork and take the payment for the first and last month's rent. That okay with you?'

Emily nodded. She'd saved well the last year, thanks to her parents' generosity.

'Good, we might as well get that done and dusted.' He headed for the front door, then stopped and turned back to face her. 'Oh, I shouldn't have to tell you this, because you do not need to go up there, but stay off the fifth floor. It's... it's currently having work done and I don't want you getting hurt.'

'No problem.'

Harry stared at her, his eyes burning into hers. 'I mean it, Miss Frewen, stay away.'

Emily swallowed and felt a chilly breeze in the room. 'I understand, I-I won't go up there... I have no need to, like you said.'

Seeming to be satisfied with Emily's reply, Harry nodded, turned away and left the apartment for the paperwork.

Once she could hear Harry walking towards the lift, Emily raised her hands in the air and squealed with excitement.

Chapter 3

THREE WEEKS LATER

The last few weeks had been spent moving in and decorating, not that Emily had much furniture to fill her new apartment with. But she did enjoy painting the walls the colour *she* wanted, and not having to endure Josh's disapproving face.

After splitting with Josh, the cheating dick, Emily had gathered her clothes together in a couple of suitcases and had left him with everything; the TV, fridge-freezer, washing machine, everything. Even though she'd purchased half of it all, she hadn't wanted to take anything with her. All those items would only carry a memory she'd sooner forget, and they weren't worth the hassle of arguing over who kept what. She just wanted the bastard out of her life.

Spending nights alone in the new apartment had felt strange at first, the quietness had felt uncomfortable, and, on some occasions, Emily would wake in the early hours of the morning after hearing distant mumbling, or her name being called. She would put this down to her mind playing tricks on her as she adapted to her new home. Being in her thirties, Emily felt a pang of embarrassment that she had never lived alone before. She was living at home with her parents up to the age of twenty-eight, when she and Josh had found a place to rent. After signing the lease for Hollow Tower, a small part of her had even felt nervous. The idea of being all alone, having to pay the bills on one income, worrying if something went wrong with the electricity, the water, the risk of break-ins and having her possessions robbed or trashed. But all those silly thoughts disappeared after her first week, when she realised how peaceful living alone can be.

Like most Fridays, Emily left her apartment with a chirpier spring in her step, eager to get to the office and have the day over and done with. Then the weekend would be hers! Netflix, snacks, wine and a sofa all to herself.

The lift arrived on the fourth floor and the old doors rattled open. Emily stepped in and pressed the button for the ground floor.

'Hold it, please!' a quiet voice called, and Emily stuck her arm out, stopping the doors from closing. A short black woman left the apartment that was on the opposite wall from Emily's, next to the door for the stairs, closed her front door and walked over.

Other than one day last week, this was the second time Emily had bumped into her new neighbour. The first was as she and the elderly woman passed in the corridor, however her neighbour was speaking on her mobile phone, and Emily hadn't wanted to disrupt her call so only smiled.

'Thank you,' the woman nodded as she stepped into the tight space. 'Oh, you're the new woman in flat twelve.'

'Yes. I'm Emily,' Emily smiled. 'I moved in a few weeks ago.'

'Nice to meet you, Emily. I'm Jasmine. Jasmine Dale. You wouldn't normal see much of me during the day. I'm a vampire, you see.'

Emily chuckled and kept her gaze as the lift moved between

floors.

'I'm joking, love,' Jasmine laughed, tapping Emily's arm. Jasmine had a warm laugh and kind eyes, the face you knew belonged to a good person. 'I just sleep through the day. I spent half my life working the night shift at a hospital, so I'm usually awake while everyone else is asleep.'

'Oh,' Emily nodded. 'I was going to hang some garlic by the front door.'

Jasmine laughed and tapped her on the arm again. Then silence fell between them, so Emily thought of what to say next. She studied the board with the buttons for each floor and examined the space for the missing fifth floor. 'It's weird that it's missing,' Emily nodded as her fingers reached out and felt the gap.

Jasmine's joyful smile dropped. She looked at the missing button space and then back to Emily. 'Harry should have told you before signing the lease to stay off that floor.' Jasmine stated, the tone of her voice now much harsher.

'Yeah, he did. I just find it strange that they'd remove the button, is all.'

'Well, they've done that because it's dangerous up there,' Jasmine argued and then added, 'It's riddled with asbestos and God knows what else.'

'It's having work done, right?'

'Yes... work to... to *remove* the asbestos.'

Emily would never describe herself as being good at reading people, but she liked to think she knew when someone was lying to her. She was sure this woman was as her words sounded unconvincing, and the quick change in her demeanour looked unnatural, like she was keeping a secret.

'Why remove access to the floor, thought?' Emily asked,

pushing the woman on the subject.

'B-because...' Jasmine began, and when the doors opened on the ground floor, she hurriedly stepped out into the lobby. 'It... it has exposed wires all around the corridor. Like I said, just be sure to stay away from it.'

Then Emily watched as Jasmine rushed off, passing Harry without saying hello as he checked his mailbox. Emily watched her neighbour push through the main doors and disappeared down the street.

'Morning, Emily,' Harry called before coughing. 'Are you settling in okay?'

'Good morning. Yes, I'm getting there. The building is extremely quiet. I love that you can-'

'That's good,' Harry interrupted and turned to face her, wheezing as he spoke. 'What were you and Mrs Dale speaking about?'

The landlord was a chubby man with little hair around the side of his head, grey stubble and heavy bags under his eyes. He stared at Emily with a look of concern on his face, and it caused her to feel uncomfortable.

'Oh, nothing much. She was telling me about the asbestos on the fifth floor.'

It was only a flicker of his eyelids, but Emily noticed it. She realized mentioning the fifth floor having asbestos problems was the first Harry had heard on the subject.

'Yes,' Harry nodded, not wanting to stay in silence for too long. He acted as though he knew what she was speaking about. 'Awful stuff. I did mention to you the day you came for the viewing to stay-'

'Away from the top floor, I know,' Emily quickly answered. 'I have no intentions of going up there, Harry. I was just curious why the button was missing.'

Harry looked down at the letters in his hand, shuffled them to check if they were addressed to him or his wife, and began back for his apartment. 'I removed the button once I knew of the... the asbestos problem, in case someone wanders in off the street, Emily. If they're hurt up there, I'll find myself in a legal battle and potentially paying court fees that I can't afford.'

That explains it, Emily thought, but still didn't fully believe him.

'Well, I have a bus to catch,' Emily nodded and headed for the main door. 'Have a nice day, Harry.'

'Yes... you too, Miss Frewen.' Harry wheezed.

Outside, Emily turned back to look in the lobby and found her landlord was still standing by his door, watching her. Then he turned and went inside.

Chapter 4

'Drinks tonight, girls?' Chloe asked around the canteen table that had many Tupperware boxes, empty crisp packets and cans of Coke scattered about. 'I need something to look forward to. This place has drained the life out of me this week.'

Emily didn't answer. She was busy chewing the ham and cheese sandwich she'd brought for lunch. Besides, spending Friday evenings alone in her apartment has become her new favourite thing. Her workdays were spent watching the clock until she could get home, kick off her shoes, take a long soak in a hot bath and then settle on the sofa.

'Where are you thinking of heading?' Hannah asked, still chewing some chicken from her salad. She quickly added, 'I'm not going back to that dark club on the other side of town that you took us to last month. That place was filthy.'

'If that's where you're thinking, you can count me out!' Amy snapped, holding up her hands. 'I must have gotten groped at least a dozen times in there. Every time I turned around, I could feel someone's hand on my arse. It was horrible.'

'What's the problem? I liked it in there,' Chloe began and then winked. 'They had hot bar staff.'

'Well, of course *you* liked it in there,' Amy began with a smirk on her face. 'You're a complete slut. The rest of us aren't.'

Chloe laughed but didn't deny it.

'Yeah, they had hot bar staff, but extremely overpriced drinks...' Hannah chuckled. 'Anyway, it doesn't matter how overprice the drinks are, we wouldn't be able to go there tonight... not with Amy, anyway.'

Amy stared at Hannah with wide eyes and an open mouth, she chuckled and then asked, 'And why not, bitch?'

Hannah looked down at Amy's chest and raised her eyebrows.

Amy had dropped some of her dinner down the front of her white blouse, and the tubes of pasta had left a tomato stain two inches long. 'Oh, God!' she called, trying to wipe it off with a napkin. 'That's just my luck.'

'Looks like you'll have to head home first and change,' Chloe stated, finished the last of her Coke and placed the can back down. 'Wait, I have a *great* idea.'

Emily, Hannah, and Amy all waited for Chloe to reveal what she was thinking.

Chloe turned to face Emily. 'How about we all head to yours tonight?'

'Mine?' Emily scoffed, trying to not sound too disappointed. She really was looking forward to lazing on her new sofa with a glass of wine and a take away, throw on a classic comedy film and fall asleep early.

'Yeah,' Chloe shrugged her shoulders. 'With Amy's blouse looking as though it belongs to a child in primary school, and not to mention that I haven't seen your new apartment yet... I figured it could be fun?'

'I'd be happy doing that,' Hannah confirmed. 'It will save us all money, too. No standing outside in the cold, queuing up!'

'But... it's... I'm still in the middle of decorating, and my living room is a mess.' Emily tried, hoping the women would change their minds and suggest some place else.

'Oh, come on,' Chloe pleaded. 'We'll have a girl's night in, it'll be fun.'

With Chloe, Hannah, and Amy staring and awaiting her answer, Emily sighed and agreed to it. 'Sure, why the hell not?'

'Yay,' Chloe cheered, flinging her arms around Emily's shoulders and pulling her in close for a hug. 'I still have Monopoly in the back of my car, from when I went camping with my niece last weekend. I'll bring that along!'

Emily smiled, trying to look excited about the plan and thought, *There's always next weekend.*

* * *

When the working day was over, the four women had all shared a taxi to Hollow Tower. They stopped on the way for vodka, wine and snacks. Chloe and Hannah had left their cars at the office, saying they'd collect them over the weekend, or leave them until Monday evening.

With all of them squeezed into the compact lift, Hannah ran her fingers over the empty square of the missing fifth floor button and chuckled, 'Unlucky for poor sods who live on the top floor, am I right?'

'Yeah,' Emily laughed, carrying one of the carrier bags with the vodka and lemonade in. 'It would be very unlucky, but it's empty. The entire floor is having work done, apparently.'

'And they want the construction team to take the stairs?' Chloe asked. 'That's harsh.'

Emily thought back to this morning, when her neighbour, Jasmine, went cold and evasive. Then there was Harry, and not just that. In the last three weeks Emily hadn't heard a slightest sound coming from upstairs. Either the construction team was strangely quiet, or they hadn't yet started the work.

'I suppose taking the stairs helps those hot construction guys to build up more of a sweat.' Chloe winked at Emily. 'You lucky bitch.'

When the doors of the lift closed, Emily braced herself for the sudden jerk that would shortly follow. Amy gasped as the mechanism began and the lift moved.

Emily said, 'I should have warned you all about that. Sorry.'

'You think?' Amy smiled. 'I hate lifts, but I hate taking the stairs more.'

They reached the fourth floor and stepped out onto the corridor as Peter Dunn, Emily's next-door neighbour, was heading towards them.

'Hey, Emily,' Peter called and waved at the other three women.

'Hi, Peter,' Emily replied as she searched in her bag for the apartment keys.

'So, *you're* Peter,' Chloe began, clutching the monopoly box in one hand as she ran her free one through her hair. 'Emily has told us *so* much about you. You're all she goes on about in the office!'

'Chloe!' Emily sighed, shooting her friend a wide-eyed stare, feeling her face burning up and turning red. She should have known better not to tell her friend about Peter. It was sometime last week when Chloe had asked if the building had any eye candy and Emily had gone into conversation about her new neighbour. Nothing in depth, just mentioning that he was handsome and easy on the eyes.

'Oh... she's been talking about me?' Peter asked, looking back at Emily and smirking. 'What has she been saying?'

'She's joking,' Emily blushed, shaking her head before pinching her work colleague on the back of the arm. 'We're having a few drinks tonight, so if any of these get too loud, just give me a bang on the wall and we'll quiet down.'

'Give you a *what* on *where*?' Chloe shouted, and Hanna and Amy both laughed, causing Emily to blush even more. She turned away and headed in the direction of her apartment. 'Ignore her, Peter!'

Peter laughed and began for the lift. 'Have a good night.'

They started with a glass of wine each, as Emily showed them around the apartment. Then, sometime around seven p.m., they ordered pizza, listened to some music, and began playing the game. Around nine-thirty p.m., Monopoly was finished with Amy stating she was no longer in the mood for playing, followed by Hannah, who had been on her phone all evening, messaging her boyfriend and hardly paid any attention to anyone.

The only alcohol left was a quarter bottle of vodka and two bottles of beer. Hannah and Amy said they were going, stumbled out of the building and shared a taxi home. Emily and Chloe finished the alcohol and Chloe was ready to fall asleep, her head dropping to her chest before jolting awake again. Emily offered her the sofa for the night, but Chloe refused, saying she'd rather wake up in her own bed tomorrow morning and not have to worry about heading home with a hangover.

'It's almost eleven,' Emily said after checking the clock. 'Just stay the night and go home tomorrow.'

'No... I'm going home!' Chloe argued.

'Taxi should be here in five minutes,' Emily said, placing her mobile back on the coffee table. 'Are you sure you don't wat to stay here for the night?'

'Positive,' Chloe smiled and burped. 'You won't be able to ride Peter while I'm here.'

Emily laughed. 'Come on, we'll head downstairs and wait.'

They left her apartment and stood at the lift, pressed the button and waited. No noise of the motor starting or from the gears as they kicked into action. Emily pressed it again and still nothing happened. 'Looks like we'll have to take the stairs,' Emily sighed and pushed through the door that led to the stairs. 'You know how impatient these taxi drivers can be. They cancel the job if you're not out within two minutes.'

Out on the stairwell, Chloe stopped at the steps leading up to the fifth floor. 'It's so dark up there.'

The corridor on every floor had a round lamp secured to the wall that produced a harsh glow. Only the bulb leading to the fifth floor was out, leaving the staircase in complete darkness.

Chloe pulled her mobile out of her bag and activated the torch. 'I wonder what it's like up there. I bet those hot construction guys are all sleeping up there, just waiting for a couple of girls like us to go up and help them out.'

'Jesus, you're such a slut!' Emily replied, then added, 'It's probably a mess from all the work going on.'

Emily headed down the stairs, but stopped when Chloe wasn't following behind her. 'Chloe?'

'It's locked,' Chloe's voice was low and distant, as she was further up the staircase.

Emily turned, took the steps back up and then proceeded up the few that led to the fifth floor. She found Chloe standing at a door that was secured by a rusty padlock, a sign stuck to the front that read **STAY OUT!**

'Look at the dust on this thing!' Chloe said, running her finger across the handle and holding it out for Emily to see. 'I thought you said it's having work done?'

'That's what I've been told,' Emily shrugged her shoulders. 'Come on, you'll end up missing your taxi–'

Chloe nudged her shoulder against the door and the wood around the lock splintered away, braking easily.

'Chloe!' Emily roared, staring at her friend in shock. 'You can't go round damaging things just because you want to see what's inside. I live in this building, you know!'

'You saw the state of that wood. It's so old. What do they expect?' Chloe scoffed and pushed the door open. They both held a hand up to their noses and winced as a foul smell of mold hit them.

'Wow, it stinks up here,' Emily moaned, stepping back. 'I can't believe you broke the lock, Chloe. If the landlord finds out, he'll revoke my lease and I'll be back at my parents.'

'Oh, get over it,' Chloe rolled her eyes and stepped into the corridor. 'He will not find out. Besides, he's lying to you.'

'What are you talking about?'

'Look at this place, Emily,' Chloe began, shining the torch-light of her mobile in Emily's face. 'There's no construction work going on up here. So, what is he hiding?'

'Well, maybe it's due to start soon.'

'Or... he has someone locked up here?' Chloe raised her eyebrows and kept her eyes fixed on Emily's. 'Keeping a poor woman chained up for his own sexual pleasures.'

'Will you listen to yourself?' Emily sighed. 'Come on, let's go.'

'You never know. There are plenty of sickos out there.'

'Chloe, you're going to miss your taxi. Let's go back before we're caught, and I'm thrown out of my home.'

'I guess you're right,' Chloe nodded and ushered for Emily to head back through the door and down the stairs. 'Let's go back down.'

Emily turned and took the stairs, then stopped when she heard the door close, but no footsteps following behind her. She spun back around and sighed, seeing Chloe wasn't following behind. 'Damn it... You annoying bitch.'

Emily headed back up, pushed through the old, rotted door and stepped into the corridor of the fifth floor. The design was the same as the other four floors, with two apartments on the same side, then one next to the door that led to the stairwell. The décor was also similar, floral print wallpaper and cheap carpets. Only up here, everything looked much older. The wallpaper was almost completely peeled from the walls and the carpets were so badly worn you couldn't make out the pattern anymore. It looked as though it hadn't been renovated since the sixties.

Emily found Chloe standing at an open door of the first apartment, looking in.

'Chloe, you're beginning to piss me off,' she said, heading over and standing at her side. 'You're going to miss your taxi-'

'Look at this place,' Chloe smiled, still holding up her mobile, and stepped in. 'Why wouldn't they get the work done and rent it out? They're losing money!'

'I told you, that's what they're doing.'

No,' Chloe shook her head. 'This place has stood empty for some time!'

Other than a wallpaper pasting table and an open pot of paint, there wasn't anything else in the room.

'They were decorating at some point,' Emily stated, ushering to the wallpaper pasting table. 'It looks as if they just *gave* up.'

'Yeah, some hundred years ago!' Chloe laughed. 'Just look at how dry that paint is, never mind the state of the wallpaper.'

Emily looked down at the pot of paint in the corner. It had turned so hard that it resembled set concrete.

Chloe walked on towards the kitchen, and Emily was forced to follow her as she had forgotten her mobile on the coffee table and Chloe was the one with the torchlight. They entered the kitchen and examined the old worktops.

'What is that there?' Chloe asked as they stepped back into the living room, looking down at where Emily was standing.

Emily looked to the floor and quickly stepped away, off the large, dark circle of dried liquid encrusted to the floor vinyl.

'It looks like...' Emily trailed off, feeling a jolt of uneasiness gush through her.

'Do you think it could be blood?' Chloe asked, and Emily met her eyes.

'Come on, let's go. As you can see, there is no one held prisoner up here.'

'We haven't even searched the bedrooms yet,' Chloe chuckled, turned and was ready to walk on. 'Who knows what we'll find-'

'We're not searching for anything!' Emily barked sternly. 'I enjoy living here, Chloe. I will not be kicked out by the landlord for not following his rules, just because you're a nosey bitch who can't behave herself. The sign on the door said stay out. The landlord warned me to keep out, and you still-'

'Okay,' Chloe scoffed, holding a hand up. 'Jeez, Emily, we'll go.'

Emily shook her head and the two women turned and began walking for the front door.

'You know, you didn't have to bite my head off-' Chloe

screamed and there was a thud as she fell to the ground, dropping her mobile.

'Chloe?' Emily cried, following the light coming from the torch and reaching for the mobile that had landed in the corner of the room. She shone the torchlight around and found Chloe sitting on the floor with one of her legs through a broken floorboard.

'Well, don't just stand there watching me, help me get out,' Chloe demanded and Emily headed over, kneeled on the floor and eased her friend's leg out of the gap. When Chloe was free, Emily went to stand, but then stopped as her eye caught something beneath the floor. Reaching for the item, she held it up to examine it.

'Ewe, that is so creepy!' Chloe yelled, taking the tiny doll from Emily's hand. 'It's ugly, and all scratched up. What kid in the right mind would even want this thing?'

Emily took it back and surveyed it. It was extremely scratched, as Chloe had stated, but also dirty and tatty. The hair had been made from red cotton, while the face looked plastic and had one eye missing. The frilly dress that was once a white colour was now dusty, yellowed and torn.

'Give me some light,' Emily said as she held the doll closer and could see a name had been sewn onto the dress. *Paige.*

'Shit!' Emily hissed, seeing her thumb was cut and that her blood was running onto the doll. She dropped it back into the gap she had found it in and saw a splinter from the broken floorboard sticking out of her skin. 'Great... Thanks, Chloe.'

Chloe laughed. 'You can't blame me for-' she stopped as the bulb hanging from the ceiling light burned brightly, fully illuminating the room, causing her to shield her eyes. 'Em-Emily... W-what is happening?'

Emily couldn't respond. She was too busy studying the weird symbols that had been etched into the bare walls. A moment later, when it looked as though the bulb couldn't shine any brighter, it exploded, leaving them with only the dim light coming from Chloe's mobile.

Chapter 5

A hundred and seventy miles away in Sheffield, eighty-four-year-old Sadie Dunn jolted awake in her bed. She ran a hand over her face, feeling that her skin was cold, sticky, and damp. The nighty she was wearing was soaked in sweat, so she pulled off the duvet and sat up. The digital clock on her bedside table beamed brightly in her dark room, showing it was just after eleven p.m. and she'd only been asleep for two hours.

Sadie furrowed her brow and rested a hand against her chest, feeling her heart beating rapidly. She had never had trouble sleeping before, and it wasn't a nightmare that woke her. She knew that for sure. It was something else, something she couldn't put her finger on.

Sadie leaned over and switched on the lamp. The light was harsh on her eyes, given the time of night, but she had to keep them open so she could inspect every corner of her room, making sure nobody was standing there, watching her.

She didn't know to explain the feeling, just that something was wrong. Something was off in the world. Something she knew was going to cause her a great deal of misery.

Ada? she thought and stood immediately. *What if it's Ada?*

Ada was Sadie's older sister by three years. After George,

Sadie's husband, passed away from heart failure a few years ago, she moved in with Ada, who had been living alone for the last twenty years, after her partner, Helen, was killed in a hit and run.

The two women have always been close, not just because they were blood, but because they were good friends who enjoyed each other's company.

With a panic in her step, Sadie rushed down the darkened corridor and slowly opened her sister's bedroom door. Ada was still sleeping peacefully under her duvet, snoring quietly.

The sickening feeling of worry in her stomach softened a little, so she closed the door back over, headed for the bathroom, washed her face and made it back to her room. She dressed in a clean nighty, dropping the damp one in the laundry basket before lying back down on her bed, not bothering to climb under the duvet now, just enjoying the cool breeze from the open window. She left the lamp on and turned to face her bedside table, admiring the faces of her two children, her late husband, George, and then her only grandson, Peter.

Sadie smiled at the framed pictures, turned the lamp off and closed her eyes. However, she knew she wouldn't sleep any further and would spend the rest of the night in the dark, wondering what the hell was going on as she patiently waits for morning to arrive so that she could discuss how she was feeling with Ada.

Chapter 6

Emily and Chloe screamed as shards of thin glass rained down from above them. Chloe grabbed hold of Emily's arm and stuttered. 'I-I want to go n-now... I'm r-ready to go home now.'

'Come on, let's get out of here!' Emily called, and they both stood, fleeing the apartment and racing down the stairs. They didn't stop until they reached the lobby and bent over to catch their breath. The rain outside was coming down hard, pelting the glass on the main doors.

Chloe looked pale as she turned to Emily and asked, 'What the hell just happened up there, Emily?'

Emily took a deep breath before answering. 'The only thing I can think of is... maybe we brushed against an exposed wire or something. That's what caused the bulb to explode-'

'Bullshit!' Chloe objected, dropping her bag to the floor and standing with two hands on her waist. 'There weren't any exposed wires in that room, or in the kitchen. And even if there were, when do they ever cause a bulb to shine like that before exploding?'

'Well, that's what I was told earlier this morning by my neighbour, Jasmine. She warned me to stay away because of the wires.'

Chloe didn't respond and leaned her back against the wall next to the mailboxes.

Emily headed over and stood at her side. 'We're lucky to be alive. Can you imagine if we were electrocuted up there? They wouldn't have found our bodies for days, maybe even weeks.'

Chloe shook her head and continued to rub at her arms. 'I'm telling you, that had nothing to do with wires.' She stared at Emily and then whispered, 'You'd have to be stupid to believe that.'

Emily watched her friend's face and saw how petrified she looked.

'Are you okay?' she asked, and Chloe nodded back. 'Are you cold?'

'Yeah, a little... My arms are so bloody itchy,' Chloe softly replied, then forced a chuckle and added. 'I've probably caught flees from that... that ugly, hideous doll that you found.'

Emily went to open her mouth to speak, but then a taxi pulled up. The driver gave a single beep from the horn before turning on his hazard lights. 'I'll see you on Monday, Emily!' Chloe said quickly, grabbed her bag from the floor, rushed through the main doors and jogged out to the taxi, holding her handbag above her head to protect her hair from the rain. Emily watched as Chloe gave her address to the driver before turning back to face her.

Through the heavy rain, Emily could only vaguely make out Chloe's figure, and in the dark of the night and from where she was standing in the lobby, it looked as though there was someone sitting next to her friend in the back of the car.

* * *

'You had a good night, love?' the cabbie asked. Chloe looked up to meet his eyes in the rear-view mirror. Though the driver wasn't looking at Chloe's face, and he wasn't concentrating on the road either, instead he was staring at his passenger's chest.

'Huh?' Chloe asked, and he looked away, back to the road.

'I asked if you'd had a good night?'

'It was... fine...' Chloe replied, feeling uncomfortable. Though it wasn't because of the man trying to get a glimpse of her cleavage - that she was used to. Men would try it on with her all the time. She knew she was a good-looking woman and was proud of her body. She was a believer of the more skin exposed, the better, and any other night, she probably would have engaged in conversation with the taxi driver, maybe even flirted a little and acted as if he had a chance with her. But tonight, something felt wrong, a feeling she couldn't place. She turned to her right and observed the empty seat next to her, unable to shake the sensation that she wasn't alone.

'How's your week been?' the cabbie asked. He seemed desperate for her to engage in conversation with him.

'It's been okay... I guess,' Chloe replied in a bored tone and continued to watch passing cars from the window.

'Your boyfriend waiting up for you at home, is he?'

'Yes, he is actually,' Chloe lied, wanting to squash any hope the driver may have had of obtaining her phone number. The last relationship Chloe had was over three years ago, and that only lasted a month. She considered herself a party girl, one with a *lot* of friends.

She slouched back further in the seat and thought of Ben Fisher, one of her casual hook ups who she had met at a bar in town. Whenever he wasn't working, Ben was usually available to come round at the drop of a hat, and Chloe liked that. When she wanted something, she wanted it there and then. Also, without fail, Ben would bring a bottle of red wine with him, and she liked that too.

Pulling her mobile from her pocket, Chloe began typing out a message to Ben, asking if he was free and was up for some late-night fun. Then she shook her head, deleted the text and locked her mobile. She just wasn't in the mood.

Perhaps I'm getting the flu, she thought, feeling lightheaded and cold. She rubbed at her bare arms, feeling a chill on her skin.

'Here, I'll pop the heating on, love,' the cabbie said, turning a switch on the dash. A second later, a humming noise started as warm air filled the car.

'Thanks,' Chloe replied.

'Don't mention it, you ugly bitch!'

'Excuse me?' Chloe yelled, not believing what she just heard.

'What?' the man asked, looking confused as he flicked on the indicator and took a turn.

'You've just called me a name.'

'No, I said I'll pop the heating on for you.'

'No, it was after that!' Chloe roared. 'You just insulted me... Me, a paying customer!'

'I didn't say a word, love,' the driver replied, watching her cautiously in the rear-view mirror again, only this time he wasn't checking out her breasts, now his look was more of concern. He wondered if he's picked up one of those strange people that he comes across now and then. Every cabbie has them.

Chloe huffed, shook her head and spent the rest of the

journey home in silence, the driver no longer trying to make conversation with her. Stopping outside of her apartment building, she reached into her purse, grabbed a note and flung the money at the cabbie, stepped from the car and purposely slammed the door shut before making it inside. Fumbling with her key in the lock, she could hear her cat, Grace, releasing pitiful cries from behind the door, pleading for food.

Usually, Chloe would be stumbling over at this time of night on a Friday, dropping take away food along the corridor while singing loudly, annoyingly waking her neighbours. But after being in that top-floor apartment of Hollow Tower, she now felt sober. The scare was enough to wake her up, and she just wanted to be home safe.

After tipping a pouch of cat meat into Grace's empty bowl, Chloe stroked the cat's head before flopping down onto the sofa. She studied her face in the mirror that was positioned in front of her on the coffee table and shrieked.

Her reflection stared back at her, only this time she didn't see the young and beautiful twenty-eight-year-old, instead she saw a woman at least fifty years her senior. Chloe gasped and plunged forward, surveying herself. 'H-how?' she murmured, running a hand over her face and pinching at her cheeks. 'No, no!'

The skin on her cheeks was saggy and filled with acne scars, while her forehead had deep, horizontal lines running across it. She began separating the skin between two fingers and trying to smoothen it out, only for it to fall back in place once she released her hold. 'How is this... how is this even possible?' Seeing the thick, black hairs growing on her upper lip made her sob. She dropped the mirror to the table, kicked her shoes off and stood. 'What the hell is happening to me?' she whispered as she headed for the kitchen. 'No wonder the driver called me an ugly bitch!'

Grace turned her head to look at her passing owner, slowly blinked and then went back to lapping up what was left of her meat.

After spending some time in the kitchen, convincing herself she was hallucinating, Chloe returned with a litre sized bottle of vodka, slumped on the sofa and reached for the TV remote. She pressed the power button and didn't bother searching for anything interesting to watch on any of the channels. She just needed to hear someone talking, to rid of the feeling of being alone.

Unscrewing the lid from the bottle, Chloe took a hefty mouthful of the liquid, swallowed, and went to rest back against the sofa cushions, but halted. 'Ow!' she cried, placed the bottle down on the coffee table and reached for her calf, where she felt a stabbing pain pierce her skin.

Moving her hand under her the leg of her jeans, she searched for what was causing her discomfort. The rusty six-inch nail clanged against the wood as she dropped it onto the coffee table. 'What the actual fuck?' she murmured, assuming it had gotten stuck under her jeans when her leg had fallen through the old floorboards.

Not wanting to be alone tonight, she reached for her mobile again and loaded Ben's messages, then typed out another message asking him to come over. Before pressing send, she met her reflection in the mirror again, shrieked at the sight of herself and deleted it, then lied back on the sofa and drank until she passed out.

It was a little after three a.m. when Chloe, still slumped on the sofa, sat up slowly. Her eyes were closed, and her breathing was slow and regular, as if she was still asleep. For the next couple of minutes, she stayed sitting in the same position, only lifting an arm, twitching her fingers and toes and turning her head from left to right, acting as if she was getting used to a body that wasn't her own.

Grace, sleeping in the chair across the way, woke, stretched and treaded across the coffee table to sit on Chloe's lap. The cat stepped on the TV remote on her way over, switching the TV over to a channel that had no signal, causing static to fill the screen with tiny black and white dots. Chloe struggled to lift an arm and when she eventually did, she rested it down on the back of the cat's neck. Her face winced as she concentrated, and a moment later, her fingers were squeezing as hard as she could. Grace tilted her head back and took a bite at her owner's fingers. Chloe pulled back her hand and Grace ran away, hiding under a cabinet in the corner.

A thin smirk grew on Chloe's lips as she whispered in a voice that wasn't familiar to the cat, 'Come to mummy, Grace...'

The cat hissed from the corner of the room and refused to move, the way she usually did whenever Chloe had a stranger over.

Planting both feet on the floor, Chloe leaned in closer to the coffee table, reached for her makeup bag, and emptied the contents out onto the surface. Her fingers ran across the items, picking up anything they landed on. With the lipstick in her hand, Chloe flicked off the lid and began coating her lips in a wide circular motion, chuckling to herself. Next, she reached for a tube of foundation and squirted some onto her face, then, using her fingers, she smeared it all around. Her chuckle now turning into full laughter.

When she was finished and her laughing had eased, she stood, almost losing her balance and stumbling back down.

As if she was auditioning for a role of a zombie on *The Walking Dead* series, she began dragging her feet behind her and headed for the bedroom, pulling off her blouse as she went. Halfway down her skinny corridor, Chloe had to rest against the wall outside of the bathroom as she unzipped her jeans, pulling them down along with her knickers before stepping out of them. Then she unhooked her bra, tossing it to the ground.

She stopped at the bedroom door, turned and made the short walk back to the coffee table, using the walls as support not to fall over. With her eyes still closed, she began pushing aside the items from her makeup bag until her fingers came across the cold, hard steel of the six-inch nail.

She grinned and began for the bedroom again, closing the door over a little behind her. 'I'll show you hideous!'

Chapter 7

The weekend was spent cleaning the mess the girls had made on Friday night. Emily had gathered the empty bottles together, along with the pizza boxes, and took them down to the recycling bins. After that, she gave her apartment a quick tidy before collapsing on the sofa, spending most of Saturday watching whatever afternoon movie was playing at the time and falling in and out of sleep. Sunday was spent preparing clothes for work, making a packed lunch and painting some more of the bedroom.

The alarm on the bedside table rang out, and Emily slammed a hand on top of it to stop the noise. Monday morning had come round far too quickly, and she really wasn't in the mood to deal with complaining customers who'd scream down the phone at her.

She yawned and pulled off the duvet, swung her legs to the side and sat on the edge of the bed, rubbing at her eyes. That's when she noticed it.

Looking down at her bare feet, she found they were covered in dirt and dust, as if she'd been treading around a building site all night. 'What the hell?' she shrieked, moving a hand down and attempting to wipe away the dust. She stopped, brought her hand back up, and inspected the end of her dirty fingers. Under the nail of her index finger was a piece of paper. It was green in colour and had a small red marking that looked like part of a rose flower. Picking it off, she could see it was a piece of scrap wallpaper. Confused, she inspected the rest of her body and found her pyjamas were also filthy. Then her second alarm sounded, and she had to quickly dive into the shower.

Slipping on her shoes, she stood at the living room window and pulled open the curtains, allowing the morning sunshine to enter her living room. The park across the way was full of early morning joggers and dog walkers. Emily took a moment to watch them all and smiled. It really was a lovely view.

She caught sight of a woman running while pushing a pram in front of her. A man walking slowly with a dog following behind. A woman dressed in black, standing there and staring at the building. There were children running a few feet ahead of their parents, scaring some pigeons and causing them to fly away. Emily brought her attention back to the woman who was standing near the entrance. From this distance, Emily couldn't fully make out her appearance, but she could see she had grey hair, dark tatty clothes and was standing incredibly still. It was hard to say for sure what window she was looking at, just that the woman was staring at the building. Before leaving, Emily raised a hand, and the woman waved back. 'Nosey bitch!' Emily huffed and backed away from the window.

A few minutes later, she was standing at the lift and waiting for it to arrive on her floor. She heard Peter leave his apartment. He smiled as he stood next to her.

'Morning, Emily,' Peter nodded, holding a reusable coffee cup in one hand and his satchel bag in the other.

'Hi, Peter,' Emily replied and noticed his cup. 'I've been

telling myself for months to get one of those things. Honestly, commuting to the office on a busy bus without coffee is just pure and utter hell!'

Peter laughed. 'Yeah, I need my coffee in the morning. It's the only thing that gets me out of bed. Where is it you work?'

'At *Pink Motors*. I'm an insurance customer service advisor. You?'

'You know *Solar Homes*?'

Emily tilted her head to the side and thought about it. 'It's the place with the plastic Wendy house screwed to the roof.' Peter added.

'Oh, yeah! The solar energy roof things, right?'

Peter laughed. 'Yep, the solar energy roof things, that's the place. I work in the I.T. department. Nothing exciting.'

'Ahh, what job is?'

'True.'

'I hope we weren't too loud on Friday night?' Emily asked.

'I didn't hear a thing, honest. Once I'm asleep, that's it. Nothing can wake me.'

'Oh, good. That bunch can get loud once they've had a few shots.'

'It's fine...' Peter smiled, opened and then closed his mouth, as if he was readying himself to ask something, but decided against it.

When the lift arrived and the doors rattled open, they stepped in and stood in silence for a second. 'Emily?' Peter began, his face a brighter shade of pink than it was a minute ago. 'Would you be interested in... in going for a drink? Hollow Bar and Grill does amazing food, and it's only a short walk through the park!'

Emily studied his face and thought for a moment. The last relationship she had was with Josh, and he hurt her badly. The betrayal she felt after finding him in bed with that skank was heart-breaking. For a while, it made Emily consider if she'd ever date again.

Peter seems like a nice guy, she thought, *but then, don't they all?*

'Yes!' Emily blurted out before her anxiety got the better of her and she could change her mind. The idea of getting back into the dating scene has been the topic of conversation around the work canteen for the last few weeks, and she didn't want that bastard Josh to ruin her life any longer. 'That would be nice, Peter.'

'Great,' her neighbour blushed and pulled out his mobile. 'Can I get your number, then?'

They swapped numbers during the journey between floors and headed out of the building together, waved goodbye, and Emily crossed the road and headed for the bus stop. She took a quick look through the railings of the park, but the grey-haired woman in dark clothing was nowhere to be seen.

Jumping off at the stop around the corner from work, Emily slowed her walking and took her time, hoping to savour the last few moments of freedom before she reached the office. She noticed Chloe's car was in the same spot that she had left it on Friday evening and guessed she probably got a taxi to work this morning.

'I take it the party only just started after Hannah and I went home?' Amy asked as Emily made her way into the office and sat at her desk.

'Huh?' Emily replied, placing the coffee down that she'd made on her way past the canteen.

'Chloe... her shift started thirty minutes ago, and she hasn't turned in yet. I'm guessing she has one hell of a hangover!'

'I've even tried calling her myself,' Hannah added after

wheeling herself over on the office chair. 'Our prominent leader isn't too happy about it.'

'So, Chloe's spoken to Michelle?' Emily asked, tapping at the keyboard to sign into her work computer.

'Nope,' Hannah smirked and pushed herself away, back over towards her own desk.

'That's why Michelle isn't happy,' Amy began. 'She can't seem to get in touch with her. She said before that Choe could at least have the decency to call up and confirm she wasn't coming in, instead of leaving her in the dark.'

'Have you tried calling her?' Emily asked.

'Only yesterday, but I was diverted to the voicemail.' Amy shrugged her shoulders and turned away. 'What more can I do?'

Emily pulled her phone out of her bag and sent Chloe a quick message.

No way you're still hungover!

Message me whenever you wake up. X

* * *

By lunch time, Emily had felt worried. Chloe had a history of either turning up late or taking a couple of sick days a year. However, she had always informed the boss and sent her friends a private message, letting them know she was too hungover or, on the rare occasion, still drunk from the night before.

As the working day had ended, Emily was readying to log off from the work system. Checking her mobile, she found there were still no messages from Chloe. She also checked the social media app she'd sent her a message on earlier, but that showed it was still unread. She dialled her number again, hoping she was awake and out of bed, but the phone only rang and then went to voicemail.

'I might stop by,' Emily said, pulling on her coat.

'Stop by where?' Hannah asked, shooting her a quizzical look.

'Chloe's place... It's weird that she isn't answering any of my messages.'

'Knock yourself out, girl,' Hannah shrugged.

'Will you come with me?' Emily asked and saw the subtly shoulder drop from her work colleague. 'It'll only take us a minute.'

'I... I have a class at the gym. Sorry.'

Emily caught Amy darting through the office and called her name.

'Bye, girls!' Amy shouted back, waved and quickly exited.

'You must know something is off,' Emily continued. 'Chloe *always* answers her mobile. The thing is practically glued to her hand.'

Hannah sighed, rolled her eyes and said, 'I can... I can drop you off on my way to the gym, I guess.'

'I'd appreciate that. It saves me waiting for the bus.'

Through the rush hour traffic, the journey took them twenty-five minutes to reach Chloe's apartment building.

'Make sure you tell Chloe that I was the one who dropped you off. She knows I would have come up, but I have-'

'The gym, I know,' Emily said and stepped out of Hannah's car. 'Thanks for the lift. I'll inform Chloe of your concern.'

The intercom panel at the front door had buttons for over a hundred apartments. Emily pressed the buzzer for number eighty-two and waited. She remembered the number from when she, Hannah and Amy all met here for drinks a few years back, before heading out to an Italian restaurant for Chloe's birthday.

The intercom beeped, signalling the call had gone unanswered, so she tried again. When this proved pointless, she pressed a random button and waited.

'Hello?' a man's voice called.

'Hi, I've just moved into the building and forgotten the pin for the front door. I was wondering if you could let me in?'

A second later, the heavy steel door buzzed, and Emily pulled it open. She took the lift to Amy's floor and gave a mighty knock on her apartment door. 'Chloe, it's Emily... I've just come by to check if you're alright?' she called through the wood.

From behind the door, Emily could hear the low cries of a cat's meow. She knocked again, and after hearing no movement from inside, she tried the handle. The door was unlocked and as she pushed it open, she could see the apartment was in complete darkness. A ginger cat ran between her legs and darted out, taking off down the corridor. 'Shit!' Emily hissed and went to chase after it. Then stopped and turned back, thinking if Chloe was by her side, then the cat would be more inclined to come back to its owner rather than a stranger.

'Chloe?' Emily called as she stepped into the living room and flicked on a light. 'Your cat has escaped, sorry!'

Chloe's living room looked messy; the TV was on, showing the black and white static, the curtains were closed and the clothes that she was wearing on Friday evening had been thrown everywhere. On the coffee table sat an open litre size bottle of vodka, with only a quarter of the liquid left inside. Next to this was a small mirror and a makeup bag with the contents sprawled out across the coffee table. With the lids missing, it looked as though every brush, foundation, and concealer had been used.

A light switched on further down the hallway, in Chloe's bedroom, and it grabbed Emily's attention. She turned her head and could see the door was slightly ajar, with shadows dancing along the wall, caused by somebody moving inside.

'Chloe, didn't you hear me knocking?' Emily asked, heading down the thin corridor. 'We need to go get your cat.' She noticed the cat's food and water bowl were completely dry, explaining the feline's pitiful cries. 'I've been calling and messaging you all day-' she stopped, heaved and held a hand up to her nose, fighting the urge to vomit. The smell that lined her nostrils was revolting. It smelt like rotting meat.

'Chloe?' Emily called, trying to bypass the smell and continue. 'Jesus, what is that smell?'

Chloe didn't answer.

Emily walked further and pushed the bedroom door open. Stepping inside the room, she saw the skinny lump under the white duvet sheet. 'What are you doing under there?' Emily asked, shaking her head. 'And why aren't you answering my messages?'

'Emily?' Chloe whispered from under the duvet. Her voice sounded faint and scared. 'Emily, help me, please.'

'H-help you?' Emily asked as she walked further into the room, grabbing a corner of the sheet and yanking it off. 'What do you need help-'

She froze on the spot, her brain trying to make sense of what she was seeing. Her eyes were unable to look away, unable to even blink. Chloe was lying naked. Her face was covered with poorly applied makeup, as if she'd let a young child practice their beauty skills on her. Her eyes bulged from the sockets and her tongue protruded from cracked lips. The colour of her skin was a mixture of purple, grey and green. Words were scratched onto her skin in thick gashes, covering almost every visible inch of her body.

The words spelt: *UGLY. DISGUSTING. VILE. HIDEOUS.*

The same words Chloe had used to describe the old doll they had found Friday night in the apartment on the fifth floor.

Chloe's arms were at her side, the tips of her fingers crusty with dried blood. The tool used to make the markings on her skin had been pierced into her throat–it was a rusty six-inch nail.

Unable to stomach the horrific scene any longer, Emily turned to walk away, but her mind was fuzzy, and she stumbled and fell against the wall, then landed on her knees. She tried but failed to stand, so instead she began crawling from Chloe's bedroom.

She had to get out of this place.

Finally, she made it back down the thin corridor and then through the living room, all while her body shook with fear and disbelief.

Before she reached the front door, she turned her head back in the direction of the bedroom and saw the light switching off, casting the room back into darkness.

'Emily, help me, please,' a voice that sounded like Chloe's softly called out from the dark.

Emily felt her eyes water, and she suddenly became woozy, causing her to drop to the floor on her stomach. Lying in the gap between the front door and the corridor, Emily called out for her friend once more. 'Chloe?'

'No... this isn't Chloe,' a deep, unknown voice replied. 'But you'll be seeing her soon!'

Unable to fight it any longer, she closed her eyes and passed out.

Chapter 8

'Miss, are you okay?' a man's voice with a thick Scottish accent called out and when Emily opened her eyes, she found she was sitting with her back resting against the wall that faced Chloe's front door. A paramedic was kneeling in front of her, and behind him stood a dozen police officers and crime scene investigators entering the apartment. 'Can you hear me?'

'I'm... Yes. I'm-' Emily tried but couldn't finish what she was saying. The image of Chloe's body came back to her, and she felt her stomach tighten with the threat of vomiting.

'Is she the one who found the body?' a tall woman with dark hair, wearing black stilettos, grey suit pants and a thin navy-blue jumper asked as she stood behind the paramedic.

A heavyset, balding man, who was much shorter than the woman and wearing a black suit and long grey coat, nodded. 'Yep, that's her.'

'Mind if we have a word?' the woman said, tapping the paramedic on the shoulder. He stood and stepped away and the woman came in closer and squatted. 'What's your name?'

'Em-Emily... Emily Frewen...'

'I'm Detective Lorna Michaels. This is my partner Detective Karl Davies,' the woman pointed behind her and the man held up a meaty hand. 'A neighbour found you lying on the floor earlier. She went inside to speak with the tenant and saw... She called us right away.'

'Chloe... she's... she's...'

'What were you doing here, Miss Frewen?' Detective Michaels asked.

'I work with Chloe...' Emily shook her head and swallowed. 'I *worked* with Chloe... She hadn't turned up at the office today and not returned any of my messages either, so I got worried and want-wanted to check in on her...'

'Fair enough,' the detective said, and then asked, 'Can you describe to me how the place was when you arrived?'

Emily looked at her and shrugged her shoulders.

'Did anything seem out of place to you?'

Emily shook her head.

'Was anything broken?' the detective asked. 'Was the door closed fully?'

'I... I haven't been here much, only once... but it-it looked *normal*. Yes, the door was closed. I knocked and when she... she didn't answer, I tried the handle, let myself in.' Tears began Emily's cheeks, and she wiped them away.

'You didn't see anyone leave?'

'No,' Emily confirmed. 'I don't understand.'

'What's that?' Detective Michaels asked.

'Chloe... she... she asked me to help her.'

The tall woman turned her head and shot her partner a confused look, then looked back at Emily.

'Did she ask you this over a text message?'

Emily shook her head. 'No. It was before I... before I pulled the duvet off her, s-she asked me to help her.'

Detective Michaels only stared for a brief moment and then

said, 'That's impossible, Miss Frewen, because your friend has been dead for at least two days, going off the signs of decomposition.'

Emily was ready to protest and tell them about the bedroom light switching on and then back off again. But that would have only caused her more trouble. The voice she had heard calling her name had belonged to Chloe, hadn't it? So, hearing the detective say Chloe has been dead for two days, it just didn't make sense.

'Do you know if your friend had any mental health issues at all?' Detective Davies asked.

Emily looked at him and shook her head. 'No. Chloe... she seemed... *happy*. She was always laughing and joking-' Emily broke out crying.

'Alright,' Detective Michaels rubbed at her arm. 'We'll need a full statement from you, but in the meantime, is there anyone you'd like us to call for you?'

Emily pulled her mobile from her pocket and opened the *recent calls* tab.

Chloe's name was at the top of the list, from where Emily had tried calling her earlier that day. She scrolled down a little and stopped on Peter's name as a nauseous feeling rushed through her and she almost dropped her mobile. The detective took the phone from her hand, inspected the screen, and passed the mobile to her partner. '*Peter neighbour*?' she asked but didn't get a response. Emily had her head resting in the palms of her hands, waiting for the sick feeling to pass.

* * *

It was thirty minutes later when Emily's mobile rang and Detective Michaels, still having hold of it, answered and gave the person directions to inside the building. Emily was sipping a bottle of water, given to her by Chloe's neighbour, the woman who had found her passed out, and who had coaxed Chloe's ginger cat, Grace, into her apartment. She had told the detective she would take care of it until Chloe's family come and claimed it.

The lift doors opened, and Peter stepped out, making his was down the corridor.

'Peter?' Emily asked, confused at seeing him there.

'This is the person you wanted me to call, right?' Detective Michaels asked.

'I... no... Yes, it's fine. Thank you,' Emily said as Peter stepped over. His eyes darted about the place, inspecting the people in white overalls enter and leave the apartment.

'Emily, what's going on?' he asked, looking at her with concern.

Before Emily could answer, Detective Michaels spoke up. 'She can fill you in later. Are you okay getting her home?'

Peter nodded.

'Miss Frewen, we may have more questions for you, so don't leave the country. I'll be in touch.'

Emily and Peter headed out of the building and over to Peter's car. In the most accurate detail she could, Emily spent the car ride home explaining what had happened. Peter had looked at her awkwardly when she mentioned hearing Chloe's voice call out for her from under the duvet, but it wasn't in a judgemental way, the way the two detectives had studied her before.

'And the light switched back off when you had left?' Peter asked as he parked the car at the side of Hollow Tower, in the private car park. 'And spoke in a... a deep voice?'

'I know, Peter, I know it sounds... *crazy*, but I swear to you–'

'I believe you, Emily,' Peter said at once, resting his hand on top of hers. 'There are forces in this world that don't make sense. Things that people choose not to believe exist. It doesn't mean they're not real.'

Emily didn't know how to react to that comment, so she nodded and exited the car.

'Thank you for believing me. I thought perhaps I was going insane.'

'No, but I understand why you didn't tell the detectives about the light switching on,' Peter said as they made it to the main entrance. He opened one of the double doors for Emily to step through. 'They'd think you were insane–'

'Emily... Peter,' Harry, the building's landlord, wheezed as he and another woman were standing in the lobby. Harry had a brush and shovel in his hand and was sweeping together some dirt. The woman next to him, who had thinning grey hair, wide eyes and a mousy demeanour, was wiping down the surfaces with a damp cloth. Harry fixed his gaze on Emily, and seeing her mascara had run down her cheeks, he asked, 'Emily, are you alright?'

'I'm fine, thank you, Harry,' Emily confirmed. 'Peter picked me up... I... I... had a fall at work, that's all.'

Peter shot her a quizzical look, curious to know why she would lie.

'And you called Peter to come get you?' Harry asked, raising an eyebrow before going back to his sweeping. 'It's none of my business!'

'Hey, Margaret,' Peter said, addressing the woman near the metal post-boxes along the wall. 'How are you?'

The woman turned to him, nodded and shot Emily a quick smile before lowering her head again.

Stepping into the lift, Emily hit the button for the fourth floor.

'Who is that woman?' she asked in a low voice, once the lift had finished rattling and they were moving between floors.

'Margaret, Harry's wife. Harry inherited this place from his father about fifteen years ago. He and Margaret both care for the building together, though it's mainly Harry who deals with the day to day running of things. I'm surprised to see her out of the apartment. She usually never leaves.'

'Does she speak?' Emily asked.

Peter sighed, turned to face her and said, 'No, she doesn't, but that's a story for another time. You don't want to hear it now; you've already gone through enough today.'

Emily didn't press him on it any further and they spent the rest of the lift ride in silence.

'Well, if you need anything,' Peter began as they stood outside of Emily's front door. 'Just give me a knock, or a call. I'm in for the rest of the evening. I'm not going anywhere.'

'Thank you again... for coming for me. It really means a lot,' Emily said, unlocked her door and stepped into the apartment.

Emily, help me, please.

Emily heard Chloe's pleading voice crying out, followed by the image of her disfigured body flashing before her eyes. 'Peter?' Emily called instantly, and stepped back out into the corridor, catching her neighbour before he entered his own apartment. 'I'm sorry... but do you want-' tears ran down her cheeks and she quickly wiped them away. '*Would* you please sit with me a little longer? I keep seeing Chloe lying there on her bed and I... I just-'

'Of course,' Peter agreed, offering Emily a warm smile. 'I

know I wouldn't want to be alone after seeing what you had.'

They spent the evening sitting on the sofa, drinking tea and talking about everything and anything. It hadn't mattered what the conversation landed on, as long as it kept Emily's mind busy and off Chloe.

Peter had ordered them both a take away, and not long after the movie they were watching had finished, Emily dozed off.

It was gone ten p.m. when Peter checked his watch and decided it was time for him to head home. He stood and reached for a blanket to drape over Emily. She stirred as he covered her with it and asked, 'Are you going?'

'Yeah, I best get back and have a shower,' Peter whispered back, pulled over his shoes and slipped them on. 'If you need anything at all, call or knock, okay?'

'Thank you for today. You're a great guy, Peter.'

He chuckled, reached into his pocket, and pulled out his apartment keys. After fiddling with the keychain ring for a moment, he placed a key down on the coffee table. 'That's my spare key, just in case you can't get hold of me. I'm a very deep sleeper, so if it's urgent, don't hesitate to come next door and wake me up.'

'Thank you,' Emily slurred before falling back asleep.

Peter crept out and quietly closed over Emily's front door.

Chapter 9

With the rain a gentle patter on the living room window, Emily, still sleeping on the sofa, sat up at once and stared directly ahead.

Though she wasn't awake, her eyes were open but not looking at anything in particular. She pulled the blanket off and moved her legs out, stood and headed for the bathroom down the hall, stubbing her little toe on a cabinet leg as she passed.

Switching on the bathroom light, she faced the large mirror and looked herself up and down, inspecting her body as if seeing it for the first time. Running a hand up her stomach, she groped one of her breasts, massaging it as a sinister smile crept onto her lips.

Turning away from the mirror and exiting the bathroom, she almost bumped into the cabinet that she uses to store her keys, purse and letters on. On her way through the living room, she undressed, taking every single piece of clothing off and dropping them to the floor before standing naked next to the coffee table. She reached down for the key that Peter had left. Her fingers, as if numb, fumbled and knocked it off onto the floor. Bending to pick it up, she held onto it tightly and headed for her front door, exiting and stepping out into the corridor.

The apartment facing was number thirteen, and it belonged to the retired nurse, Miss Jasmine Dale. The elderly woman had always had trouble sleeping. Working all those years on the graveyard shift at the hospitals had messed her sleeping pattern up. As Jasmine was on her way to the bathroom, she heard a door closing outside and diverted to her front door to take a peep through the spyhole.

'What in God's name...' she mumbled, seeing a naked woman pass her apartment, walking as if she was dragging her feet. She quickly unlocked her door and pulled it open. 'What are you doing prancing around naked? Don't you have any dignity?'

Emily didn't slow her walk, but turned to face her and only stared, then looked away. She reached Peter's front door, inserted the key, and quietly pushed the door open. Before stepping inside, she turned back to face Jasmine and held a finger to her lips. 'Shh!'

'You... bloody young people!' Jasmine shook her head and went back inside, closing and locking her door behind her.

Emily, still with her eyes open but not concentrating on anything around her, made her way down the hallway and into Peter's living room. A soft light shone from a tropical fish tank in the corner, the filter making a low bubbling noise. Above the tank was a shelf that housed some framed pictures. Emily headed over to it, picked up one of the pictures that showed Peter with his grandmother, sitting on a park bench with sandwiches and canned drinks in front of them, the sun beaming down on their faces. Emily frowned at the picture and dropped into the fish tank before slowly walking away, towards the bedroom where a snoring noise was escaping from. As she pushed the door open, the hinges creaked a little, but it didn't seem to interrupt the sleeping man under the duvet. Emily closed the door over and made her way to the empty side of the bed, slipped under the duvet and ran her hands along Peter's bare chest. Peter stirred a little but still didn't wake. She went a little further, moving her hands down and into the waist of his pyjama pants, grabbing hold of his penis.

'Um... you... then the...' Peter slurred nonsense. Emily moved closer, so her breasts were against his chest, and began stroking his penis faster. 'No... why are the-' Peter jolted awake and jumped back, running a hand over his face. 'Em... Emily, what are you-' he broke off and switched on the bedside table lamp. 'What the hell are you doing in my bed, Emily?'

He noticed his neighbour's eyes were open, but not focused on him.

'It's okay.' Emily's voice was low and sounded a little unclear, as if she was drunk. 'I want this... I want you.' She shifted closer to him and moved her hand below again.

'Stop this!' Peter ordered, pushing her hand away. 'What are you playing at?'

'I know you... you w-want me too...' she managed and leaned in to kiss him.

'Are you... sleepwalking?' he asked, avoiding her kiss, and stood from his bed.

'I'm the best you-you're ever going to-to get,' Emily mumbled, moving herself across the bed further and kneeling in front of him, trying to kiss his chest. 'Take the opportunity while you can.'

'Emily, stop... I mean it!' Peter shouted and pushed her away again. Emily lost her balance, stumbled to her side and fell off the bed, landing on the floor with a thud. She moaned and held a hand up to her head. '

What are you....' She trailed off, blinking and looking all

around before placing a hand on the bed and standing. 'Peter?' she asked, staring at him and then down at her naked body. She screamed and pulled the duvet off the bed to cover herself. 'What the fuck, Peter?' she hissed, backing away from him. 'What were you trying to do to me?'

'*Me*?' Peter scoffed with a shocked expressed. 'It was you who came in here, naked and trying it on.'

'Don't you dare!' Emily hissed, jabbing a finger at him. 'I wake up and find myself in *your* room! What did you do, drug me?'

'What?' Peter yelled, his breathing becoming harsh. 'You looked as if you were sleepwalking and got yourself in my bed-'

'Oh, piss off, Peter,' Emily shook her head. 'I have never slept walked in my life, not even as a child.'

'Well, you must have been-'

'I'm going to the police...' Emily started for the bedroom door. 'You're sick and need to be locked away.'

'The police?' Peter scoffed. 'You can't be serious?'

'You spent the evening with me, pretending you cared and were being friendly after I discover Chloe dead, and now I wake up in your room without remembering how I got here? I'm sorry, but I don't do that sort of thing.' She pulled the door open and marched down the hallway, struggling to keep the duvet up to her chest.

'Emily, I'm telling you-' Peter tried.

'Fuck you, pervert,' Emily shouted back, and exited the front door. 'You took advantage of me when I was vulnerable. I can't believe you!'

Emily walked down the corridor towards her own apartment as Peter chased after her. 'Stay back, Peter, I mean it!'

A second later, they heard a door unlocking, and Jasmine Dale stepped out. 'What the hell is going on out here?'

'Jasmine, will you call the police, please?' Emily said. 'This man just tried raping me!'

'Are you drunk?' Jasmine asked, causing Peter and Emily to both fall silent and stare at her. 'I asked if you were drunk?'

'What? No, I'm not drunk,' Emily replied in a tone as if she'd just been insulted. 'I woke up in this man's bed and I have no recollection of how-'

'No, you didn't!' Jasmine grunted and crossed her arms.

'Excuse me?' Emily huffed, holding the duvet higher up her chest.

'I watched you walk right past my door only what... two minutes ago.'

'What?' Emily said, feeling sick at the thought.

'Yep. You walked right past looking directly at me, inserted the key in the door and then turned back to face me and said "Shh."'

'I-I did?' Emily asked, swallowing and looking from the elderly woman to Peter, who now had an angry look on his face.

'You thought I could do something like that?' he asked and shook his head. 'You know where to find me when you're ready to apologise,' Peter grumbled and walked back to his front door. He turned to his neighbour and nodded. 'Thank you, Jasmine.'

Then he was gone. His door slammed shut.

Feeling embarrassed, Emily quickly turned and darted into her own apartment, swinging the door closed behind her. She noticed the clothing she was wearing earlier that day was now scattered around the living room floor.

Did I actually sleepwalk? she thought, dropped Peter's duvet and began dressing. Making it to the bathroom, she splashed some cold water onto her face, looked up at the mirror and screamed. The reflection staring back at her wasn't her own.

For a briefest second, her face had sagged, her hair was thin and grey, and she was dressed in black tatty clothes. The strange woman in the mirror shot her a thin-lipped smirk, then was gone. 'I'm losing my fucking mind!' Emily mumbled, turned and headed for Peter's apartment, grabbing the duvet from the floor on the way.

* * *

After knocking quietly, Peter answered a few seconds later, holding a pair of tongs.

'Yes?' he said in an annoyed, flat tone.

'I'm... I'm sorry,' Emily apologised, shaking her head. 'I must have slept walked. I think seeing Chloe earlier has made me... I don't know.' She began crying and Peter held his door open wider.

'Come in,' Peter offered, taking the duvet off her and heading into the living room. He dropped it on the chair in the corner and walked over to the fish tank, placing the tongs into the water and retrieving the framed picture of him and his grandmother.

'What are you doing?' asked Emily, stepping into the room and taking a seat on the sofa.

Peter held the picture up as water dripped off it. 'This ended up in there... somehow.'

'Did it fall in?'

'Not a chance,' Peter answered, plucking a couple of tissues from a box and patting the picture dry. 'I keep it on the shelf here,' he pointed to an space on the end of the shelf. There were two other pictures situated before the space, one of his parents and the other of him, sitting on a canal bank fishing. 'So, it's impossible for this one to have fallen in before these two.'

'Well, how do you think it got in there, then?'

He looked up and met her eyes, but didn't reply.

'You don't think... that it was *me,* do you?' Emily asked, feeling guilt rush through her. 'Peter, I would never-'

'Like you'd never sleepwalk and bring yourself into my bed?'

Emily stayed quiet.

'It was on the shelf earlier on,' Peter continued. 'I know that because I fed the fish once I came home.'

'Why would I do that?' Emily rubbed at her face. 'What is happening to me?'

'You've had a hard day,' Peter replied, placing the picture down on a cabinet and made his way to the sofa to sit at her side. 'Finding your friend de- Being the one to discovery her must have been hard on you. It would be hard on anyone.'

'It wasn't just that she was dead, Peter,' Emily sighed, resting back on the sofa and picking at her fingernails. 'It was the *way* I had found her... The mess she was in. All those words sliced into her skin, then hearing her call out to me. I can't stop thinking about it. I can't seem to get her voice out of my head. It doesn't make any sense.'

'I know.' Peter rested a hand on her arm. 'It's obviously playing on your mind, causing you to sleepwalk. Not that I've ever heard of anyway sleepwalking after experiencing something awful, but I guess we all grieve in our own way.'

Emily nodded. 'I guess so. I hope the police find whoever did this to her!'

'What makes you think it wasn't suicide?' Peter asked, stood and headed for the kitchen. 'You want tea?'

'I'd love a cup. Maybe Chloe killed herself. Maybe she was dealing with demons I did not know about.' Emily held up a hand, shaking her head. 'I just didn't think she'd do such a thing. Friday night, after we finished drinking, fooling around upstairs and she went home, I should have contacted her. I should have checked in on her the next morn–'

'What did you say?' Peter asked, coming back out of the kitchen in a hurry. He stood wide eyed with a wary look on his face. 'Emily, what did you just say?'

'That I should have checked in on Chloe–'

'No,' Peter shook his head and darted across the living room. He grabbed hold of Emily's shoulders and squeezed them tightly. 'What did you just say about being upstairs? Do you mean the fifth floor?'

'Ow, Peter, you're hurting me!' Emily shrugged, breaking free of his grip, and nodded. 'Yes, we... Chloe and I were fooling around upstairs before she got a taxi home. I know it's out of bounds and I wasn't supposed to be up there. It was just a bit of fun.'

Peter stood staring at her; his face had turned pale, and he looked as though he was ready to pass out. 'You shouldn't have gone up there, Emily,' Peter murmured, running a hand through his hair. 'You really shouldn't have gone up there.'

Chapter 10

'What's the problem, Peter?' Emily asked, feel a little frightened.

'I'll... I'll go make us that tea...' Peter sighed and turned for the kitchen. 'You're going to need it.'

He returned a few minutes later and sat back on the sofa next to Emily. 'Where do I begin? The fifth floor isn't really having work carried out.'

'Well, yeah, that's obvious,' Emily huffed. 'I'm not stupid. It's been weeks and I haven't heard a single sound from up there.'

'Harry and Margaret tell the new residents that to keep them out. It should have been locked up.'

'It was locked. Chloe busted it open with her shoulder.'

Peter frowned and shot her an annoyed look.

'I know, I know, but she was so drunk. So, what is up there that they don't want anybody to see?'

'A spirit,' Peter said with a serious face, and waited for Emily to respond.

'A spirit? Really, Peter, come on?'

'You told me earlier that you heard Chloe's voice calling out to you?'

'Yeah,' Emily nodded, slapping a hand against her thigh. 'My mind was playing tricks on me… I-I had a shock after finding my friend's body in that awful state.'

'You also told me it was before you entered the bedroom,' Peter replied quickly. 'Then the light switched on and back off again. Nobody else was in the room, right?'

'Yeah, but…' Emily trailed off and shrugged her shoulders. 'You don't… you can't jump straight to the conclusion that it's down to ghosts, Peter.'

'Then what do you think?' Peter asked.

'I don't know… Maybe after smelling that awful stench coming from her room, that I subconsciously knew what I was expecting to find and my memory of how the light was switched on became a little… *hazy.*'

'Hazy? I doubt that.' Peter replied, pulling a mug of tea closer, raising the cup and taking a sip. 'There are good spirits and evil spirits in this world, Emily. Most of the time… people… regular people would never encounter one, but they're there. Sometimes we can hear them shout, other times we can't, and we'll walk right through them knowing no different.'

Emily thought back to her first day in the apartment, when she came for the viewing and heard a voice call her name, only then to receive a cautious look from Harry when she answered.

'The spirit upstairs, Mary Anne, is evil,' Peter fell silent for a moment, thinking and then he continued. 'Or so I've been told. Years ago, after an incident with her daughter, Mary Anne made a promise that, whoever moved onto the fifth floor, she would make sure they were hurt. I can't remember exactly how the story went, but for years after, families were put through misery. Mary Anne caused some havoc up there. She would bring people to commit suicide and act out… *insanely.* It was my grandmother who put the spirit at bay.' Peter stood, walked over to the picture frame that had retrieved out of the fish tank and handed it to Emily. 'That's my gran Sadie. She and my grandfather, George, had lived here since the sixties, then when he died a few years back, she moved in with her sister Ada and I took over the place.'

'You look like her,' Emily smiled. 'You have the same eyes.'

'I've been told that before,' Peter nodded and attempted a smile but couldn't. 'She was the one who told me everything that had gone on up there. It makes sense now.'

'What makes sense?'

'Why I found that picture in my fish tank.'

Emily only looked at him and furrowed her brow.

'My gran studied witchcraft. She was the one who performed a spell that bounded the spirit to ever leave the fifth floor. I'm guessing Mary Anne didn't like her very much after that.'

'When did your grandmother cast this spell?' Emily asked, sipping at her tea.

'It was about ten years ago now. The top floor was closed off for years by Harry's late father. After he died and Harry inherited the building, he and Margaret got tired of losing money...' Peter drank more of his tea, placed his mug down and continued. 'An entire floor with three empty apartments just sitting there collecting dust. That's some money wasted, wouldn't you say?'

Emily nodded. 'Yeah, it's a real waste.'

'Harry and Margaret wanted to open it up again, have people move in so they could make some money. They figured perhaps Mary Anne had moved on, so they started to redecorate... Only things didn't go to plan and Margaret was hurt... hurt bad.'

'Go on,' Emily prompted him to continue, even though she

knew she would not enjoy the story.

'Harry asked for Sadie's help. He, Margaret, and my grand-parents took an enormous risk entering that place again. They searched the highs and lows of upstairs, but they couldn't find what was allowing Mary Anne to continue to exist here, in our world.'

'What do you mean?' asked Emily, shaking her head. All this ghost talk was new to her.

'In order for Mary Anne to continue... *existing*, there must be something anchoring her to this world, our world! An item she loved or had a strong connection to in her past life. Anyway, Mary Anne knew exactly what they were doing up there that day. She knew that if they found and destroyed it, she'll be gone for good.'

'So, what happened?' Emily asked, eager to learn more.

'Whatever it was they were searching for, they didn't find it. So my gran cast a spell to lock the spirit inside whatever the item was, and like most spells, they can be broken. She had told me later that a single drop of blood would release the evil spirit from the hold.'

'Shit!' Emily sighed, holding a hand up to her face and pinching the bridge of her nose as a sickening feeling entered her stomach.

'Yeah, it's a crazy story, I know-'

'No, it's not that. I mean, the story is insane, but...' she swallowed and took a moment to continue.

'But?' Peter said.

'But... I may have found what it was Mary Anne had been hiding up there.'

Peter stared at her, shifted on the sofa so that he was facing her head on and asked, 'What did you find, Emily?'

'Friday night, when Chloe and I were upstairs, she fell, and her foot went through this broken floorboard in the living room. I had to help her yank it out, and that's when I found this old, creepy doll. It had a name stitched on the dress that read–'

'Paige!' Peter moaned, and Emily felt a shudder run up her spine.

'Yes! How-how did you know that?'

'Paige was Mary Anne's daughter who died. Where did you find the doll?'

'Un-under the floor,' Emily answered, looking pale. 'I picked it up and noticed my finger was bleeding, so I dropped it back into the hole. It should still be there.'

'We need to tell Harry; he'll want to hear about this.'

'Peter, we can't. Please, don't tell Harry!' Emily begged, grabbing hold of Peter's hand. 'He warned me before I moved in not to go up there. I don't want to lose my home. Even if there's a crazed ghost living on the top floor.'

'He'll know soon enough, Emily. I don't know how, but we need to have Mary Anne locked away again. None of us are safe while she's out.'

'What about your gran? Can't she help again?'

Peter shook his head. 'I don't feel comfortable asking her. The last time she performed that spell she was in her seventies. She's almost eighty-four now. What if it's all too much for her and she's hurt? I'll never forgive myself.'

Emily thought for a moment. 'You said everyone was looking for this item, the doll, right?'

'Yeah.'

'What if we go up there, find it and bring the item to your gran? We can have her cast the spell and send this *spirit* on.'

'If we have the doll, then a spell isn't needed. All we'll need to do is set fire to the thing. It will break the chain that's keeping Mary Anne here. We might not to have to tell anyone about it at all, including Harry.'

Emily swiftly stood, placed her mug down, and said, 'Let's go now.'

* * *

'We should probably wait for the morning, right?' Emily asked, as they made their way up the dark stairs. Peter was in front, holding a torch that he had brought along.

'If we leave it till the morning, who knows what might happen? Your friend Chloe, I'm guessing Mary Anne had something to do with her death, going off the horrific way she was killed. How you came into my room earlier, what if that's connected to Mary Anne?'

'You're right,' Emily agreed. 'The sooner, the better, then!'

Peter stopped before opening the door that Chloe had forced open a few nights before. 'We need to be quick in here, Emily. Where exactly was it you found this doll?'

'First apartment on the right, broken floorboard in the living room.' Emily answered at once. She was carrying Peter's metal bin from his bathroom, a box of matches and a can of lighter fluid.

'On my count,' Peter said, with his hand resting on the door, ready to push it forward. 'Three. Two. One!' he pushed the door open, and he and Emily rushed down the dusty corridor and into the first the apartment. 'Stay close to me!' Peter called, turning back to check Emily was behind him. 'In and out. I don't want to be part of a story people are talking about years from now. In and out. Okay?'

'Okay!' Emily agreed, feeling woozy at the excitement of it all, or perhaps the fear. She was supposed to be enjoying living in her new apartment - chilled evenings spent watching TV, drinking wine and relaxing - not dealing with all this supernatural troubles.

They made it into the living room and Peter located the broken floorboard. He raced over shining the torchlight inside. Then turned back to Emily, panting with a look of shock on his face. 'Was this the place that you found it?'

Emily nodded. 'I dropped it back into the gap, Peter.'

She came closer, peering into the gap herself, and found there was nothing but dead insects, dust and splintered wood.

'Where's the doll?' Emily shrieked. 'I left it here!'

Peter swallowed, held a hand to his head and muttered, 'Shit... '

Chapter 11

They took the stairs to the ground floor and knocked on apartment 2 - Harry and Margaret's door - the building's landlords. A moment later, Harry answered, wearing a bathrobe fastened around himself and a pair of battered slippers that had seen better days. As his chest wheezed, he shot Peter a concerned look, then glanced at Emily and moved his eyes back to Peter. 'Not again,' he sighed as a concerned look made its way onto his face. 'Tell me the pipes in the bathroom haven't burst again, Peter!'

'I'm afraid it's more serious than that, Harry,' Peter swallowed, lowering his gaze to the floor. 'A hell of a lot more serious!'

The landlord stepped aside and pushed the door open. 'You best come in then.'

The three of them walked into the living and met Margaret who was sitting in one of the armchairs facing the TV. She was in the middle of knitting a child's hat and stopped when she saw Peter and Emily enter the room. A look of dread fell upon her face. Harry came into the room and Margaret stared at him for answers. Harry held out his hands, showing he didn't know the reason for their visit, and ushered his tenants to sit on the sofa.

The landlord's apartment was crammed with trivial clutter. There was no doubt the couple were hoarders. In one corner, there were boxes piled high with different board-games. In a glass cabinet next to the sofa, Emily noticed the shelves were filled with tiny porcelain figurines. Behind the chair that Margaret was sitting stood another cabinet that had three old TVs resting on top.

Margaret reached to the side of the chair and grabbed the Magna Doodle, a children's magnetic drawing board that had an eraser, operated by sliding it across to clear away the image. She spelt out the words, *WHAT IS IT*?

Peter sighed, darting his eyes from the couple facing him. 'She's... she's out.'

Harry and Margaret looked at each other but didn't speak a word. Margaret shook her head as tears suddenly fell from her eyes, rolling down her cheeks.

'Mary Anne?' Harry asked with a quiver in his tone as he turned back to Peter.

Peter nodded. 'Yes, her.'

With a trembling hand, Margaret slid the bar across the bottom of the magnetic drawing board, erasing her last message, and quickly wrote another. *HOW*?

Taking a second to answer, Peter looked to his side and shot a glance at Emily. Margaret knocked a knuckle against the board, grabbing his attention and demanding he answer her last question.

'It-it was my fault,' Emily answered quietly, sounding as though she had lost her voice. 'My friend and I... We-we went up there on Friday night, we were drunk and fool-fooling around. I'm very sorry.'

'Jesus,' Harry sighed, staring at her with tired eyes. 'I told you to... No, I *warned* you to stay off the top floor–'

'I know.' Emily nodded, refusing to look at him. 'I know you did. I'm very sorry. I tried staying away, but my friend headed up and I followed behind her.'

'Have you spoken to your friend since?' Harry asked, scratching at his face and creating a rasping noise from his stubbly cheeks.

Emily stayed quiet, lowered her head, and kept her gaze fixed to the floor. 'She's... um...'

'I'm afraid she's dead, Harry,' Peter chimed in, resting a hand on top of Emily's shaking knee. 'Emily's friend is dead.'

Harry looked at his wife. Margaret had her eyes closed and was still shaking her head from side to side. Harry asked, 'Was that why you were looking so stressed earlier on?'

Emily nodded as tears rolled down her cheeks. 'Chloe was a good person; she didn't deserve to die like that!'

'Can I ask what happened to her?' Harry said.

Peter turned to Emily. 'Do you want me to tell them what you told me?'

Emily nodded again and picked at her fingernails.

'After Emily finished work, she had gone to her friend's apartment to check up on her. Emily told me earlier that her friend had called her from the bedroom, asking for her help. Only when Emily entered the room, her friend was lying dead under the duvet. Words had been scratched into her skin, made by a steel nail that was pierced into her throat.'

Margaret made a whimpering noise and Harry sighed, rubbing at his face again.

'The police had said that she's been dead for at least two days,' Peter continued. 'But Emily swears she heard her friend's voice calling her name, then a light was switched on and off again.'

Margaret jotted another question down on her magnetic drawing board and turned it around for them to see. *WHAT WORDS?*

'I believe they were ugly, disgusting, vile, and nasty.' Peter answered.

'*Hideous*.' Emily corrected him. 'Not nasty. Hideous!'

'Sorry,' Peter nodded. 'Her friend was lying naked under a duvet with...' he turned to face Emily again, 'did you say the words were across her entire body?'

Emily nodded. 'Almost, at least all over her chest, stomach, arms and the top of her legs.'

'That's awful!' Harry murmured, shaking his head.

'They were the words that Chloe had used on Friday night to describe the doll we had found up there.'

Harry and Margaret both jolted in their seats and shot each other a look. Then Harry quickly leaned forward in his chair. 'Did you say doll?'

'Yeah. We found an old doll that belonged to Paige,' Emily confirmed, she coughed to clear her throat, and continued. 'Peter tells me Paige was Mary Anne's daughter and–'

'Yes, that's correct. But, Emily, where is that doll now?' Harry asked, staring at her with a desperate look in his eyes.

'We don't know, Harry,' Peter answered as he slapped a hand against the top of his thigh. 'We went up there before, hoping to find and burn the damn thing. But it was gone.'

Margaret let out another low whimper and Harry hissed, 'SHIT!'

Margaret cleared her last message, wrote another, and tapped Harry on the arm. In scruffy writing, she had written, *ITEM?*

Harry nodded. 'It has to be, love. It has to be!' Margaret nodded back and Harry faced Peter and Emily again. 'Ten years ago, Margaret and I wanted to redecorate the top floor,' Harry began, and even though Peter had vaguely discussed this earlier, Emily didn't want to interrupt him. 'It was a Sunday; I'll always remember that because we agreed to have a roast dinner after we finished up there.' Harry looked over to Margaret and she smiled at him. 'We thought we'd tackle Mary Anne's apartment first. Margaret was sweeping up and getting the tin of paint ready whilst I was scraping away the old wallpaper. That was when I saw those markings on the wall. My father had warned me about Mary Anne years ago. He told me she was a witch. A dark one. People who had moved into that apartment had complained to my father, telling him it didn't matter how many coats of paint they'd used to cover up the symbols written on the wall, the paint just wouldn't stick. So, luckily, the residents settled for wallpaper. When I came across those symbols, I decided to try something new, so I reached inside the toolbox for a utility knife and ran the blade across the bottom of one of the symbols. I figured if I couldn't paint over it, I'd try to scratch it off the walls instead. Once I made the first cut, I had to drop the knife to the floor; the handle had felt as if it was on fire. It was so hot that it left a thin red line across the palm of my hand. Then the lights flickered, shining so bright they burned our eyes, as if we were staring directly at the sun. We had to shield our faces from it. That was when *she* appeared.' Harry paused, staring down at the floor as he remembered the day. 'Mary Anne stood there, in the corner, smiling at us with a wide grin as if she had something to be proud of.'

Emily looked over at Margaret and could see she had her eyes fixed on her husband, tears still rolling down her cheeks.

'I stepped forward,' Harry continued, 'telling her to leave. That this is our building, and she wasn't welcome any longer.

That she'd already caused too much grief and misery for innocent people over the years. She just continued to stare, smirking at us. Margaret stepped forward and jabbed the brush broom towards her, ordering her to leave us alone. Mary Anne held out her hand, facing her palm towards Margaret, sending her flying against the wall witch such force that she had the air knocked out of her. I could see she was trying to move but couldn't, as if there was this invisible barrier restricting her. I tried to head over to help, but Mary Anne lifted her other hand and I fell to the floor. My knees had completely given up, refused to work. The only way I can explain is that it felt like I had this heavy blanket covering me, keeping me pinned down. Anyway, Margaret shouted, "You evil bitch, leave us alone" and from the look on Mary Anne's face, you could see she didn't like that. She didn't like it one bit! Her grin had turned mean, and she sprinted towards Margaret, then vanished inside of her. Margaret was able to step away from the wall, but her movements weren't her own. The way she walked, her strides, they weren't natural. She was acting like a puppet, as if she was being controlled by someone pulling her strings.'

'What happened then?' Emily asked, eager for him to finish the story.

Harry continued. 'Margaret stepped over and picked up the utility knife off the floor. I could see smoke leaving her hand as the handle burned into her skin.'

Margaret lifted her hand and turned it around. Emily almost gasped at the sight. The skin on her palm was twisted and looked like leather.

'At first, I thought Margaret was going to kill me. She stepped in front of me, holding the utility knife up to my throat. I could see she was fighting Mary Anne's force, or, at least, she was trying to. I could tell from the look in her eyes as she stared down at me that Mary Anne was inside of her. All I could do was watch it play out. The only thing I had control over was my eyes, I could blink and move them left to right, but that was all. I couldn't speak or move; I couldn't help my Margaret–' Harry broke off, crying and wiping tears away.

Margaret leaned over and rested a hand on his arm. When he looked at her, she nodded, ushering him to continue. Harry got himself under control and spoke some more. 'That *bitch* Mary Anne was enjoying it, I could tell. Then Margaret knelt in front of me, reached into the toolbox for some pliers, stared into my eyes and said, "This will teach your wife to speak out of line to me!" I watched as Margaret brought the pliers up to her mouth, using them to hold out her tongue. Then she used the utility knife to slice it off. I'll never forget Margaret's screams as her blood filled the floor. But she didn't stop, not until she had sliced through the whole thing and was holding it up in the air. I couldn't help her...'

Margaret opened her mouth and showed Peter and Emily the stump where her tongue had once been. Emily had to divert her eyes to stop herself from puking as she pictured the gruesome scene. Peter shifted in his seat, and it was clear that he was extremely uncomfortable, too.

Emily thought back to Friday night when she saw the dark stain on the floor in the living room. Now she knows that was Margaret's blood.

'It was my fault,' Harry sobbed with a look of shame on his face. 'I was warned by my father to stay away from that floor, but I didn't listen. I got greedy. I wanted to make a profit from those empty apartments.'

Margaret wrote on the magnetic drawing board and stroked

his arm to get his attention. *NOT YOUR FAULT!*

Harry smiled at her before turning back to face his two residents. 'That was when we turned to Peter's grandmother and asked her for help. It was no secret that Sadie was a witch. Everyone in the building knew it. Some believed her spells worked, some didn't. But after coming face to face with Mary Anne, seeing Margaret hurt that way, I was willing to try anything to get rid of that bitch. Sadie had agreed to help us and asked if we had anything personal that belonged to Mary Anne, but we couldn't find anything. Sadie explained to us that there must have been something up there that helped Mary Anne continue to exist, but after seeing what she had done to Margaret, we couldn't risk searching the place thoroughly. That was why all Sadie could do was cast a spell to keep her bound to that item... to the doll!'

'Jesus,' Emily murmured.

'Yep,' Harry wheezed. 'Even after Sadie's spell, I couldn't risk allowing families to live up there, in case they came across it, and Mary Anne would be released again. I would be the one responsible for their deaths.'

Emily lowered her head, feeling guilty for not forcing Chloe down the stairs and away from the fifth floor. If only she hadn't allowed her friend to go up there, Chloe would still be alive, and there wouldn't be a wicked spirit controlling people.

Margaret erased her last message and wrote out another. She tapped her knuckle on the board to gain Harry's attention. *WE NEED TO FIND IT!*

'We can't, love,' Harry protested. 'We can't risk going back up there, not without help. Look what she did to you last time, and you've just heard what she did to Emily's friend!'

Margaret tapped on the board again and added another

exclamation point at the end of her message.

'I want her gone just as much as you, Margaret,' Harry huffed, and then turned to Peter. 'Do you think your gran would help us again?'

Peter sighed, he wanted to tell him he wasn't going to ask. But how could he say no? A malicious spirit has been released in the building, and it needed to be stopped. Mary Anne needed to be stopped.

'*If* I ask her, and she says no, then what do we do, Harry?'

'Then we're fucked, Pete...' Harry muttered, staring at him. 'If Sadie can perform that spell again, it will keep Mary Anne at bay long enough for us to search that apartment. It must be in there somewhere. We can't go up there searching about without Sadie casting the spell. I'm surprised she didn't kill the two of you before.'

Peter and Emily both looked at each other and then back at Harry.

'Now we know what we're looking for,' Harry continued, 'maybe it'll make it easier. Maybe we can finally send that bitch to hell once and for all.'

Peter nodded, looked at Emily and then back to the building's landlord. 'I'll drive to Sheffield tomorrow and ask her. I think it would be best breaking the news to her in person that Mary Anne has escaped.'

Margaret tapped at her drawing board and when Peter looked over, she shot him a sincere smile to say thank you.

'Can I come with you?' Emily asked.

'Don't you have work?'

'No way am I going into the office tomorrow,' Emily stated. 'Not after finding Chloe. Besides, I don't think I want to be here alone... not now, after learning what she's capable of.'

'That's understandable,' Harry sighed, and in a low voice, he added, 'Even if it is your fault that she's out.'

A slapping noise was heard as Margaret whacked Harry on the arm and then gave him a stern look.

'Sure, you can come with me.' Peter nodded.

'So, the doll belonged to her daughter,' Emily began. 'What happened to her?'

'When Paige died,' Harry began, standing and heading off to the cabinet behind Margaret's chair, the one with the old TVs on. 'That was when Mary Anne *really* went off the rails. I have a picture of the two of them here somewhere.'

Harry opened the bottom drawer of the cabinet, moved something aside and pulled out an old shoe box. He took off the lid, searched through a couple of letters and then pulled out a black and white Polaroid picture that had curled at the sides. He handed it to Emily and said, 'My father wanted a shot of all the residents that summer, so he could have that picture hung in the lobby.'

Emily studied the polaroid. It had a date written on the bottom, but she couldn't make it out due to the ink that had been smudged. It showed over thirty people standing outside of Hollow Tower; men, women and children, and from the way they were dressed, it looked to have been taken in the sixties. Emily studied the photograph, taking in all the residents' faces and stopping on one in particular. Harry leaned in closer and held a finger out to point. 'That's Mary Anne, standing there-'

'This one!' Emily interrupted, pointing to a smiling woman that had her hands resting on a young girl's shoulders that was standing in front of her. Emily had to strain her eyes because of the quality of the image, but she could see the little girl was clutching onto a small doll.

'Yes,' Harry confirmed, shooting her a cautious look. 'How on earth could you possibly know that?'

'Because she's the woman I saw... in the mirror.'

Chapter 12

'You saw her?' Peter asked. 'When was this, Emily?'

She felt nervous having Peter, Harry and Margaret all stare at her as they awaited her answer, like she was on trial at a courthouse, giving a statement.

'It was after I got back from your apartment,' Emily answered, swallowed and went back to looking at the image in her hand. 'I splashed some water onto my face in the bathroom and when I looked up, she was there, in the mirror... watching me. At first, I thought I was going insane, that perhaps I was still in shock after finding Chloe, but now it makes sense.'

'Maybe you didn't sleepwalk,' Peter nodded. 'What if, like the way she controlled Margaret that day, she had controlled you too?'

'Sleepwalk?' Harry asked.

Peter glanced at Emily, and she subtly nodded, giving him the go ahead to tell them what had happened earlier on. 'Emily slept walked into- She *made* her way into my room earlier, climbed into my bed and was... well, let's just say she became very touchy... Anyway, I had to push her off, but she doesn't remember doing it.'

'I *wouldn't* do that sort of thing!' Emily scoffed. 'You're a good enough looking guy, Peter. But I wouldn't force myself on you like that. I have some dignity.'

'It was Mary Anne,' Harry said and rested back in his chair, causing the old furniture to creak under his weight. 'It was one of the ways she would split families apart. I remember when I was a boy, Mr Kevin Hickling, a schoolteacher and an all-round gentleman, lived in apartment seventeen, Mary Anne's old place. He lived there with his wife, Maxine, and their young son, Joseph. One night, Kevin broke into the apartment facing. At the time, there was a young woman living there, alone. She woke up to him trying to rape her, catching him yanking her top up as his free hand tugged at her pyjama bottoms, trying to force them down. The woman managed to push him off and ran out into the corridor, screaming for help. Maxine had heard the screams and saw that her own front door was unlocked and standing open. She ran out to investigate and found her husband standing there with his trousers around his ankles, asleep. The police came and Kevin had told them he didn't remember leaving his bed, and that he had no experiences of sleepwalking. Of course, he was arrested and awaiting trial...' Harry trailed off, a saddened expression fell on his face as he stared at the floor.

'Harry?' Peter said, pulling him from his daze. 'What happened to the Hickling family?'

'Kevin... he hung himself. Left a note to his wife, stating that he couldn't go on with people thinking he could do something like that.'

'Fuck me,' Peter whispered.

'Yeah,' Harry sighed. 'Maxine was found a week later, sitting in a pool of her son's blood after cutting his throat as he slept. She tried to plead that she didn't know how she had gotten hold of the straight razor and found herself in Joseph's room, stating that she must have slept walked. Maxine was sent to an asylum and died a few years later, so I was told.'

Emily felt a cold shiver run through her and she fought the temptation to rub at the goosebumps coating her arms.

'A month later, in apartment sixteen, the one further down, a man named Richard Belton had moved in. Richard lived alone and in his free time, he liked to paint. He was a very talented man, I believe. I heard that, out of the blue, Richard had quit his day job and refused to leave his apartment. There were paintings of Mary Anne stuck to every wall in every room, as if he was obsessed with her. Richard would tell the other residents that it hadn't mattered where he travelled to, he would see Mary Anne's face wherever he went. That he wasn't obsessed with her, and it was more that she was haunting him. There was an unfinished painting of a grey-haired woman in black, tatty clothing, standing across the way, on the other side of the railing, inside the park. It was obvious that it was Mary Anne, and in the painting, she had solid black eyes, her index finger sticking out and curled as if she was beckoning him over. As with the rest of the portraits around his apartment, Richard had painted her with that same wide, sinister grin, stretching from one ear to the next. My father discovered the painting on the easel later that day, next to the window Richard had jumped from.' Harry shook his head. 'There are more stories like this, but I won't go into them now. I will say though, every one of them ends in death and misery, and every one of them involves Mary Anne.'

'I saw her from my living room window too,' Emily admitted in a low voice. She coughed and spoke a little louder. 'She was dressed in those black tatty clothes, like in Richard's painting, and she was waving at me. It was only this morning, before my day turned upside down, and I learned Chloe was dead. I thought nothing of it... I just assumed it was some nosey old lady in the park.'

'She's made a connection with you, Emily,' Harry sighed with a look of fear in his eyes. 'That's how it happens. She gets under the person's skin, makes them believe they're going crazy, weakens them... that's when she strikes... forcing you to harm either yourself or someone else.'

'What do I do?' Emily asked with a tremble in her voice.

'We need to have Sadie perform the spell before she has the chance to make you do something terrible.' Harry answered.

Peter rested his hand on top of Emily's again. 'You'll be okay. We'll make sure nothing happens to you.'

Emily smiled, though she didn't believe him. Hearing the stories about what had happened to the Hickling family, and then Richard Brenton, she wasn't sure they could do anything to protect her against that sort of evil.

'So, what happened to her daughter, Harry?' Emily asked.

Harry swallowed and darted his eyes away for a second, as if he was embarrassed to tell the story. 'My father was doing his rounds and had witnessed Paige playing about in the corridor. Moments later when he reached the ground floor, the electricity was shut off. The entire building lost power and there was a huge scream from the top floor. When my father made it up there, he saw Paige had stuck an old nail she had found in one of the wall sockets, electrocuting herself.'

'How...' Emily began and altered her question. 'Without sounding harsh here, how is that anyone's fault but Mary Anne's for not watching her daughter?'

'Exactly,' Harry nodded. 'But Mary Anne blamed my father,

said it was his building and that the socket was faulty. Anyway, Paige died shortly after, and Mary Anne took my father to court. She lost the case and even though it was awkward for him, he didn't ask her to leave. How could he? The woman just lost her daughter.'

'What did she do then?' Peter asked.

'From what I remember, she began drinking heavily,' Harry confirmed. 'I knew, before Paige's death, Mary Anne and Sadie would often sit in the park, or visit each other's apartments as they studied witchcraft together, but she became a recluse, shutting people out who had once meant something to her. She kept herself locked away, drinking and chanting from books. I'd often go up there and listen through the door. I could hear her late at night, shouting words that didn't make sense to me. The only time I would see her was when she crossed the lobby, leaving the building for more booze while clutching hold of that doll.' Harry leaned forward, finished his cup of tea, and continued. 'I remember waking in the early hours of the morning to the noise of our door being pounded on. One of the residents had come down to get my father, saying Mary Anne was asking for him upstairs. I quickly followed, and we made it to the top floor to find her sitting in the corridor, drunk and mumbling a load of nonsense. My father knelt at her side, trying to help her up and that's then she slashed his face with a piece of broken glass. She began laughing hysterically, and I ran over, pulling my father away as blood ran down his face. She kept screaming, "You let her die!" My father was shaking his head, saying he wasn't responsible for Paige's death, but Mary Anne wouldn't have it. She calmed for a moment, looked him dead in the eye and said, "This floor will be cursed from now on. My blood will remain, and I will kill anyone who tries to make a home here!" Then she chants these words I couldn't make out. I think it was Latin. Anyway, once she was finished shouting, she sliced her wrists with the piece of glass and bled out in front of our eyes.'

When Harry was finished talking, the room had fallen quiet as everyone spent a moment to take in what they have been told. Emily felt sorry for what the woman had gone through. But that doesn't mean she should attack innocent people. Innocent women like Chloe, her friend.

'Best get back upstairs then, hey?' Peter suggested, and Emily stood at once. She wanted out of this room now, away from all the talk of death and misery.

They thanked Harry and Margaret and took the lift to the fourth floor.

When the doors rattled opened and they began down the corridor to their apartments, Emily turned to Peter and said, 'Will you please stay with me? I don't feel safe being alone... Not after hearing all that.'

Peter nodded. 'Only if you promise not to try anything...'

Emily slapped his arm and attempted a smile, but one wouldn't show. After everything that had happened - hearing how the little girl had died, the suffering Mary Anne had released on the residents - she didn't know if she'd ever feel like smiling again. At least not while she was living here.

'We'll stay in the living room,' Peter said as he waited for Emily to open her front door. 'Sleep in segments. I'll take first watch; you can get some sleep first. It'll be safer for us both if one of us stays awake. Keep an eye out for anything that feels wrong.'

'Right now, everything feels wrong!' Emily stated.

'I agree there.'

'You can sleep, Peter. You'll need your rest before the long drive tomorrow. Besides, I won't be sleeping at all tonight... Not knowing what danger I've released upon people.'

'Hey, you can't blame yourself, Emily. The spell that kept Mary Anne locked up was always going to be broken. If not by you, then perhaps twenty, thirty years from now when Harry and Margaret are long gone. These things happen. No one can prevent it.'

Emily managed a small smile and nodded, though his words hadn't shifted how she felt.

After making a pot of tea, grabbing some biscuits from the cupboard and settling on the sofa, they watched some cartoons on TV, hoping the childish humour would lighten their dull moods. Peter had fallen asleep an hour later and Emily stayed awake, as promised. She flicked through the pictures on her phone, showing her and her three work colleagues as they celebrated Christmas office parties and birthdays.

'I'm sorry this happened to you, Chloe,' Emily whispered, staring at her phone screen. In the picture, Chloe was holding up a jug of purple liquid, filled with ice and had multiple straws poking out the top. She was sitting on a bench in a beer garden as the sun beat down on her face. 'I'm going to make sure that bitch pays for what she's done to you!'

Chapter 13

After Peter popped next door for a quick change of clothes and a wash, they left Hollow Tower just gone eight a.m. Harry and Margaret were in the lobby and waved them off.

'You must be exhausted, Emily,' Peter said as they climbed into his car. 'You didn't drop off once throughout the night?'

Emily clicked her seat belt in place and shook her head. 'Nope. I couldn't have slept even if I wanted to. All I could think about was the way I found Chloe. What Mary Anne had done to her... She needs to pay, Peter. She needs to be punished for hurting my friend.'

'She will be,' Peter promised, placing his hand on top of hers. A moment later, realising what he had done, he quickly pulled it back and blushed. 'We'll make sure she's stopped. Don't you worry.'

Emily gave Michelle, her office manager, a call stating she won't be in work today and broke the news about Chloe's death. Five minutes later, her mobile buzzed with texts and phone calls from Amy and Hannah, though she didn't answer any of them. She didn't want to explain the gory details of how she had found their work colleague.

They stopped at a drive thru for coffee before heading for

the motorway. Once on the motorway, Peter put his foot down, hoping to gain some miles. However, they didn't get far, as thirty minutes into their journey, the lights above the motorway had signaled for them to slow down, and a couple of miles further up ahead, they had come to a complete stop. An accident involving two cars and a lorry was the cause of their disruption, and they'd already passed the exit to take another route. 'Shit!' Peter hissed as he applied the handbrake.

Emily reclined her seat and laid back.

'I was wondering when the tiredness was going to hit you.' Peter chuckled.

'I'll probably-' Emily covered her mouth as she yawned. 'Sorry. I was saying I'll probably only have twenty minutes. A quick nap usually does me.'

'Take as much time as you need,' Peter replied, finishing what was left in his coffee cup. 'We're going to be here for a while, anyway.'

It seemed twenty minutes wouldn't do Emily after all, as she was still asleep an hour later. Peter was crawling through the traffic, moving a couple of inches at a time before coming to a stop again. He had the music on low, hoping not to wake his sleeping passenger. Applying the handbrake again, he looked at Emily and thought, *She's incredibly pretty!*

Another thirty minutes later, when he had finally passed the accident and grimaced at the sight of the overturned car and the dented front grill of the lorry, he was able to put his foot down and bring the car back up to an appropriate speed. He checked the clock on the dashboard and sighed. Eleven a.m. The accident had taken a decent chunk of time from their day, and he just prayed Sadie hadn't already gone out shopping. He thought maybe turning up unannounced wasn't a great idea after all.

Looking at Emily, he watched as her fingers quickly typed at her mobile.

'Oh, you're awake. Good!'

Emily didn't answer and only continued to tap her phone screen. When she finished what she was typing, she locked her mobile and placed it in the door pocket.

'Emily?' Peter laughed. 'Are you ignoring me now?'

Emily jolted in her seat, rubbed at her face, and murmured. 'Huh?'

'I said it's good that you're awake. I need some company; I've been bored shitless on this motorway.'

Emily slowly sat up and rubbed at her eyes, blinking. 'Yeah,' she slurred and fixed her hair out of her face. 'Yeah, I'm... I'm awake now.'

'How long have you been awake?' Peter asked in a curious tone.

'Are we nearly there?' Emily asked, taking a sip of her coffee that had gone cold. She winced at the taste and swallowed.

'I'd say we have another twenty miles or so.'

Emily went quiet as she stared out the window. 'Peter?'

'Yeah?'

'What if your gran can't help us?'

Peter took a moment to answer. The same thought had run through his mind over the last couple of hours and he had forced them away, not wanting to imagine going back to Hollow Tower without Sadie at his side. 'She will, Emily. I know my gran will do what she can for us.'

'But what *if* she can't?' Emily asked, the tone of her voice now sounding demanding. 'Maybe what you said was right, that she's getting too old to be doing this sort of thing. It could be extremely dangerous for her.'

'Then... I don't know what we're going to do,' Peter answered, swallowed and ran a hand through his hair. 'I guess we'll... we'll have to leave the building.'

'That wouldn't matter. Chloe didn't live in Hollow Tower and Mary Anne still killed her. It wouldn't matter where I went, Harry said I'd made a connection with her, so she's never going to leave me alone. Not until she plays with me a little, tortures or makes me want to kill myself.'

'My gran will help us. Try not to worry.'

'I hope so,' Emily murmured.

They spent the last twenty miles speaking about other things. Meaningless things that would keep their minds occupied until they arrived at Sadie and Ada's place.

Chapter 14

Just after eleven a.m., sitting alone in the corner of *Ray's Bar,* at a wobbly table just big enough to seat two people, Josh Cooper finished the last of his beer and waved to get the barmaid's attention. With effort, Josh shot her the biggest smile he could force onto his face and held up his index finger, signalling to the young girl working the morning shift that he'll have another pint of beer. The barmaid rolled her eyes, scrunched her face and pulled a clean glass off the shelf before pouring the beer. Kayla was the girl's name, and it seemed Josh's politest smile still went unappreciated.

Kayla didn't like him. Josh knew that. Other daytime drinkers noticed it too, the way she would avoid his conversations, slam his change down onto the bar instead of handing it over, serving him last out of the queue of people waiting to be seen. And it wasn't only Kayla, it was the pub's manager and the other bar staff who disliked him. Ever since the night Josh had gotten inappropriately *handsy* with her as she tried closing for the night. After the manager had barked a stern a warning and threatened him with the promise of being barred from Ray's Bar indefinitely, Josh had apologised to Kayla before stumbling home to sleep on his father's sofa.

Any of the other nearby bars wouldn't have let him back in, but not *Ray's Bar*, because this back-alley place was a struggling dive and Josh was their number one customer, occupying a barstool at least five, sometimes six days a week if his money stretched that far.

Kayla brought his beer over and placed it on the table in front of him.

'Cheers, Kayla. It's quiet in here this morning, isn't it-'

'Do you want it on your tab or are you paying now?' Kayla grunted, standing with a hand resting on her waist, and shooting him a snobbish scowl.

'Put it on my tab, please.'

Of course, Josh could always drink some place else and receive much nicer customer service, but he's already tried the other establishments, and Ray's Bar is the cheapest in town. Being a full-time drinker, cheap is exactly what Josh needs.

The barmaid frowned and turned away. Josh went back to looking out of the small, grimy window, watching shoppers walking past on the main road further up.

Losing Emily twelve months ago was only the beginning of his misery. His life had turned upside down since. Not that he blamed her for leaving. Who'd want to stay with someone who had betrayed their trust? The day she had come home from her cousin's hen party, walked into their bedroom and caught him fucking another woman is the memory that occupied his mind daily. Though getting himself in a state of drunkenness would help him forget the pain.

The shock he saw on Emily's face that day keeps him up at night. Josh had climbed off the woman he was on top of and rushed over to speak with her, but Emily had left straight away, refusing to even look at him and headed for her parents' place, not giving him the chance make up some silly excuse as he tried to keep her. Days later, her father had turned up with a van, gathered her belongings together and left Josh with everything else. Just as she had instructed.

Weeks followed and Josh, realising the mistake he had made by cheating, hid his feelings by drinking, taking drugs and attending random parties that were hosted by strangers he'd met while out on one of his benders. It wasn't long before he stopped turning up for work and was then eventually let go, sending him spiralling into a depression and frantically searching for other employment, desperately taking on any job that he was offered. Of course, weeks later the drug fuelled weekends and one-night stands took off again, and Josh was out of another job, then another. Soon enough, unable to pay the rent and upkeep of the apartment on a temporary wage, he was forced to move into his father's one bed bungalow and sleep on his sofa. His plan of finding work and renting his own place again was soon forgotten about and now, Josh spends any money he receives from government help on booze, cigarettes and cheap drugs that give him a quick buzz.

Life is *extremely* miserable for Josh.

Josh reached for his vibrating mobile from the table, turned it around and found a number on the screen he didn't recognise. 'Not today!' he murmured, placing his mobile back down again, assuming the message would be from a debt agency, chasing him for one of his many unpaid loans. Or maybe it would be an employment agency, offering him a short-term back-breaking job for ridiculously low pay. They are the only type of messages he ever receives these days.

No one ever bothers with loser Josh. *Creepy* Josh, as he'd heard Kayla sneer occasionally.

Taking a sip of his fresh beer, he hears his mobile vibrate again, reminding him of his unread message. 'Jeez, who do I owe this time?' he sighed, grabbed his mobile and opened the messages app. As he read it, two things happened simultaneously; a spark of hope burned in his stomach, and he was quickly put off his beer. 'Shit,' he smiled, 'Oh, my... Shit!' Josh stood and raced over to the bar. 'Kayla, I'll like to settle my tab, now, please.'

The barmaid took her time to look up from her mobile. She acknowledged him and then went back to tapping at her screen again. 'Kayla!' Josh roared, slamming a hand down on the bar and making Kayla jump with fright. Right now, he didn't care if the manager wouldn't allow him back in again, if what he had just read was correct, then sitting alone and drinking himself silly would be the last thing he wanted to do right now. 'I want to pay up... I... I have to be somewhere!'

'Okay!' Kayla huffed, placed her mobile down and operated the register to prepare his bill. 'Wait, you've still got a full pint left on your table. What's the rush?'

'I won't be drinking it...' Josh grinned, forcing himself to keep his smile under control as a giddy feeling ran through him. His eyes darted left to right as he inserted his bank card into the reader. He looked agitated, and at the same time, happy and eager to leave. 'Bin it, I really don't care what you do.'

'*You*? You don't care what happens to your almost full pint?' Kayla stared at him, unsure if she heard correctly. 'Are you saying you want me to tip your beer down the sink?'

Josh chuckled a little under his breath and then said, 'I don't give a shit what you do with it, Kayla. Looking at your miserable face has put me off drinking it, you stuck-up bitch!'

He pulled his card from the machine, turned and rushed out of the pub in such a hurry he almost knocked over a man heading to the bar.

Chapter 15

Peter slowed the car down as they reached Locket Street, a quiet and leafy place with a mixture of houses and bungalows. He studied each house carefully, shook his head and drove on a little further, stopping at the next one he thought could belong to Ada.

'Don't tell me you don't know which house it is!' Emily chuckled.

'It's been a few years since I've been up here,' Peter replied, smiled and stopped outside a semi-detached two bed with a knee-high fence that had been painted Manor Red. 'We're here.'

'Are you sure it's this one?' Emily asked, unclipping her seatbelt.

'Positive. Nanna Sadie lives with her sister Ada. Ada's late girlfriend, Helen, used to have a thing for lighthouses. It was more of an obsession, if I'm being honest.' Peter replied, nodding at the front garden. The garden was small, half concrete flags and half grass. It had numerous sized ornaments of lighthouses dotted all around, each of them painted in different colours and styles.

They headed up the path, knocked on the front door, and waited. A few seconds passed that felt like minutes, and there was still no answer.

Emily shot Peter a concerned look, and he knocked again. 'Maybe we should have called her first. Made sure she's-'

The door opened and Ada, a fragile-looking woman with curly grey hair, answered. 'Peter!' she called excitedly and stepped out onto the stoop to hug him. Then she turned to face Emily. 'And you've even brought your girlfriend!'

Peter blushed. 'No, Ada... Emily isn't-'

'Come in, come in!' Ada ushered, stepping back inside and walking them to the living room. 'Sadie, you have a wonderful surprise.'

It was obvious the two women were sisters. Sadie and Ada were both short, fragile looking and had the same round shaped face. Sadie was sitting on a chair at the kitchen table, working on a thousand-piece puzzle of a Japanese garden. When she saw Peter enter, she frowned and grunted, 'Great!'

'It's lovely to see you too, Gran.'

Sadie stood and moved slowly over to greet them. 'I'm always thrilled to see you, love,' Sadie began as she kissed him on the cheek and then walked off to the sofa, leaving Peter and Emily to follow behind and take the two armchairs facing. 'But... the truth is, I was expecting you to show up.'

'You were?' Peter asked.

'Yes. You see, I couldn't put my finger on it, this weird feeling I've had all weekend. And now here you are, and it makes complete sense.'

'Tea anyone?' Ada asked and left the room before anyone could answer.

'Who is this, then? Your girl-'

'No, Gran... this is Emily, she's my... my neighbour at Hollow Tower.'

Sadie took her eyes from Emily and burned them into her grandson's. 'Yeah... that's what I was afraid of.'

'I'm sorry?' asked Emily, feeling as though she has insulted the old woman in some unknown way.

'Not that I have a problem with you being his neighbour, love,' Sadie confirmed, smiled and winked at her. 'It's about time Peter had a pretty girl living next door to him. The poor lad has had to deal with Jasmine Dale and Joyce Gibson for the last few years. The building needs more young people.'

'Miss Gibson moved out, so that's the apartment Emily rents now.' Peter explained.

'Right. Is Jasmine still there, keeping a nosey eye on people?' Sadie asked, and Peter nodded.

'Bloody woman never sleeps,' Sadie mumbled, then turned to face Emily and said, 'Let me guess. You went to the top floor, didn't you?'

Emily swallowed and slowly nodded, her eyes falling to the coffee table in front of her, concentrating on the old tea-stained coasters.

'Was this on Friday, around ooh... eleven p.m. sometime?'

Emily nodded again, remembering she had offered Chloe to sleep on the sofa around that time, but she had refused, so Emily booked a taxi.

'How... how can you possibly know this?' Peter asked.

'I could feel it.' Sadie frowned. 'I woke that night in a cold sweat and had a strange feeling in my stomach. I could feel her, Pete.'

'You could feel Emily?' Peter scoffed.

'No. *Her.* I knew that bitch Mary Anne had escaped the hold. I just didn't want to believe it,' Sadie sighed and looked back to Emily. 'Tell me how this happened...'

Emily spent the next few minutes explaining how she and Chloe had gone upstairs, explored the old apartment, then she described the state she had discovered Chloe in on Monday evening.

'I told Harry to take drastic measures last time,' Sadie hissed, sounding annoyed. 'I warned him to block off all access to that floor the last time I was there. Now a girl is dead!'

'He did,' Emily said, nervously fidgeting with the tips of her fingers. 'He removed the button in the lift and the door on the stairs was locked with signs ordering you to stay out, but we... My friend broke it open, and we entered.'

Sadie shook her head and muttered, 'You silly girls!'

Ada came back into the living room and placed a cup down in front of both Peter and Emily, then left for the kitchen again to bring one in for Sadie before disappearing upstairs.

'Has she harmed anyone else other than your friend?' Sadie asked.

'No,' Emily answered. 'But she... controlled me the other night. Had me doing–' Emily broke off as her cheeks burned a bright red.

Sadie noticed her grandson look away with an embarrassed look on his face and knew whatever Mary Anne had forced Emily to do, it had involved something sexual with Peter. 'She had you doing something you wouldn't *normally* do?' she asked, and Emily shyly nodded.

'Yeah, that sounds like Mary Anne alright. For years I've dreaded this day. I knew she would be back!' Sadie uttered with a look of unease on her face. Peter thought it looked like fear and completely understood why.

'I'm sorry,' Emily said.

'Don't apologise.' Sadie shook her head. 'It was only a matter of time until she was released from the spell. If we'd found what kept her there, we could have destroyed it and have her gone forever-'

'That's why we're here, Gran,' Peter started, shifting forward in his chair. 'Emily found what it could be.'

Sadie's mouth fell open as she stared at her grandson, then she looked at Emily. 'You-you've found it?'

'I did... I just don't know where it is now.'

'We went back up there last night,' Peter began, 'hoping to find it and burn the damn thing. Stop Mary Anne before she had the chance to hurt anyone else, but we didn't see it.'

'I swear I left it where I had found it on Friday night,' Emily protested, still playing with the tips of her fingers. 'Only last night it was gone. Someone- *Mary Anne* must have taken it. Hid it elsewhere.'

'After all these years, I've been wondering what the hell it could have been. Please, tell me what you found!'

'A doll,' Peter answered before Emily could. 'Emily said it was an old, tatty, looking thing that belonged to Paige. It had her name sewn onto the dress.'

Sadie nodded and reached for her cup. Before taking a sip she said, 'That makes sense. It was a shame what happened to that little girl.'

'What if Mary Anne had taken it and hid it somewhere outside of Hollow Tower?' Emily asked, leaning forward and reaching for her own cup.

'No,' Sadie swallowed, shaking her head. 'She wouldn't have done that. Mary Anne wouldn't risk taking it out of the building. She'll want it tucked away somewhere close by. A place she can see it. If it isn't in Hollow Tower, anything could happen to it.'

Peter said, 'At least knowing that it is definitely in the building improves our chances of finding the doll.'

'Not just in the building,' Sadie smiled. 'She'll keep it in her old apartment. I'll bet my life on it.'

Peter and Emily both looked at each and nodded.

'We'll finish our tea, then I'll pack a bag and we can make our way there,' Sadie said. 'After we deal with her, I'd like to stay for a couple of days. All that traveling in one day is too much for me. Besides, it would be nice to see the old place, the area and the people. That okay with you?'

'Of course!' Peter answered joyfully. 'It'll be great to have you staying for a while. I'm sorry that I'm asking you to do this, Gran.'

'I'm just happy I'm still alive to help you.' Sadie nodded, smiling at Peter. 'God knows what would have happened if I'd passed on and that evil bitch was released.'

'Hopefully, we can stop her for good this time,' Emily said.

'Yeah, hopefully!' Sadie agreed.

* * *

After packing a case, Peter, Emily, and Sadie headed out to the car. Emily sat in the back, offering the passenger seat to Sadie.

Ada waved them off at the door, watching as the car made it to the bottom of her road before she turned and headed back inside the house. She gathered the cups from the coffee table and took them into the kitchen, placing them in the sink with some soapy water.

CRASH!

The sound of an ornament smashing was heard from one of

the upstairs bedrooms and Ada shrieked. 'Jesus,' she murmured and headed through the kitchen.

I bet I've left that bloody window wide open again! She thought, taking the stairs slowly. Last week, Ada had left the window in the bedroom open, and as the wind picked up, it blew the curtains out and knocked a glass of water from her bedside table, sending it smashing to pieces on the floor.

As she pushed her bedroom door open, she saw her window was firmly closed and there was nothing broken on the floor.

CRASH!

Another noise sounded, this time coming from the spare room further down. Only that was impossible, as there shouldn't be any windows open in there, because Ada hadn't stepped foot in that room for months. Neither has Sadie, because she knew this room was off limits. It was the only rule Ada had given when her sister had moved in from London.

The room had once belonged to Helen, Ada's late partner, and was filled with all of her clothes, shoes, records, and her beloved crafting table. Ada couldn't stand to look at those old things anymore. The pain of losing her was too much. Occasionally, every few months or so, Ada would stand at the doorway and pop her head in, making sure a pipe hadn't burst, or that there wasn't anything else she needed to report and have repaired. Then she would close the door again, step away and sob quietly in her room.

Only now the door was ajar, and she could see a shadow on the wall inside, flickering as someone moved about. Ada felt a cold shiver run up her spine as she stood outside of it. She contemplated entering, but what could she do if she came face to face with a young man stealing her possessions? Instead, she began down the stairs to call the police and inform them she has an intruder.

'Ada?' a woman's voice called out. 'Ada, love, is that you?'

Ada froze on the stairs and turned around, tears instantly forming in her eyes. She hadn't heard that voice in such a long time. The voice that belonged to the person she had loved for over half of her life.

'Helen?' Ada called.

'Yes, it's me, Shortcake!' the voice that sounded like Helen's had replied, and even though it had a slight twang to it, Ada hadn't noticed. It's been too long since she heard the voice of her beautiful Helen that a slight difference was easily missed.

Ada whimpered and held a shaking hand up to her mouth. Shortcake was the name Helen had given her years before, due to her small structure.

Ada quickly began up the stairs, eager to see her partner again, and pushed the door open. 'Helen, what are you doing here?'

Her eyes fell on the half-painted lighthouse ornaments lying broken on the floor. They were what Helen was working on before she passed. Looking up from the floor and over to the swivel chair at the crafting table, Ada saw the back of a grey-haired woman's head. The stranger in the chair clutched onto the table with claw-like fingers and spun herself around.

'You're-you're not my Helen!' Ada mumbled.

'No,' Mary Anne smiled a wide and devious grin, reached to the floor for a shard of broken porcelain and stood. 'No, I'm not your Helen, Shortcake!'

Ada felt her knees turn to rubber as she stared into the cold, evil eyes of the thing standing in front of her. She wanted to scream and run, but she knew there was no point, she wouldn't get far. 'You're... the one they were talking about... You're the spirit tormenting Hollow Tower!'

Mary Anne slowly began walking towards her. 'Yes, and I am the one that will murder all of them.'

'No,' Ada shook her head and began backing out the door, towards the stairs. Even though she was trembling with fear, she forced a smile onto her face and added, 'My sister will stop you. Sadie will send you to hell before you can-' before Ada could finish, Mary Anne growled, rushed forward and drove the piece of porcelain straight into her neck. Ada attempted a scream before toppling down the stairs. Though it went unheard as Peter, Emily and Sadie were now over two miles away, readying to join the motorway and head for London.

Chapter 16

Joining the motorway and bringing the car up to speed, Peter held a hand to his stomach as it released a loud rumble that travelled around the car. 'Oh, wow. I'm sorry, I didn't realise how hungry I was!'

'Wait, haven't you eaten breakfast yet?' Sadie asked.

Peter shook his head. 'No. We stopped for coffee this morning before setting off. Then there was an accident and the traffic was dreadful, so I didn't want to waste any time stopping for food. Not when Mary Anne is out there somewhere, causing trouble.'

'Well, an extra thirty minutes won't kill us, will it? Let's stop at the next restaurant we see.'

Peter glanced in the rear-view and met Emily's eyes. She nodded enthusiastically and joked, 'I could eat a horse. I'm starving.'

Sadie chuckled. 'You see, even your girlfriend is... even your *neighbour* is hungry.'

Peter looked at Emily again and could see she was smirking and avoiding his eyes.

'So, then, Emily,' Sadie began, shifting in her seat to turn her head around a little. 'Tell me about yourself.'

Feeling like a kid standing at the front of the class who is forced to give a speech, Emily blushed as she thought of what to say. 'Well, I work in an office, in insurance. I love reading, even though I don't do enough of it-'

'Oh, Peter is a huge reader too!' Sadie blurted. 'He's always got his nose stuck in a book somewhere. All those science fiction alien stories are his favourite.'

Emily continued. 'I like to travel. Again, I don't do this much either.'

'Peter is always going on about wanting to travel more too. He wants to see more of the world.'

'Gran!' Peter barked and shot Sadie a stern look. 'Will you... just stop it, please!'

'Stop what?' Sadie asked with an innocent look, as if she didn't know what she was doing wrong.

'I... I know what you're trying to do...' Peter mumbled, refusing to look in the rearview mirror as he felt his cheeks beginning to flush.

'I'm not trying to do anything, Pete. I was simply asking the girl a few questions, trying to get to know her better, that's all.'

'No, you're not. You're trying to play cupid and get involved with my love life-'

'Well, if you grew a pair and asked the pretty girl out on a date yourself, I wouldn't have to get involved!' Sadie huffed.

'Gran!' Peter roared, staring at her. 'Seriously?'

Emily giggled from the backseat.

'I'm so sorry, Emily...' Peter said.

'Isn't that diner along this motorway somewhere?' Sadie asked, studying the motorway signs. 'That place we went for food when you drove me to Ada's all those years ago?'

Peter nodded and was happy for the sudden change in conversation. 'Yes, it is. It's a few more miles further yet. *Big Shirley's Kitchen*, it was called.'

'That's it!' Sadie cheered excitedly. 'Emily, they do the best milkshakes you'll ever taste. I love them.'

'Well, now I'm looking forward to trying one.' Emily replied.

* * *

Ten miles further, *Big Shirley's Kitchen* came into view as Peter pulled the car off the motorway and entered the services. Though the building wasn't what he remembered. Years ago, when he last drove Sadie up to Ada's and they stopped for dinner, the building looked enticing, welcoming even. Now, it had an old, torn banner hanging above the door that read ***UNDER NEW MANAGEMENT*** while the brickwork looked filthy and in desperate need of a clean and a fresh lick of paint. The windows were grimy and there was rubbish overflowing from the bins next to the steps that lead to the entrance. The neon sign that had once flashed *BEST SHAKES AROUND* now flickered with a couple of letters not working. To top it off, a homeless man was asleep on a cardboard box at the side of the steps with empty beer cans lining the pavement next to him.

'Jesus,' Sadie muttered as she stepped from the car and studied the building. 'This isn't the same place, is it, Peter?'

Peter nodded. 'I'm afraid so, Gran. Whoever the new management is, it looks as though they'd ran this place under. What a shame.'

'The motorway sign said that the next services aren't for another thirty miles, so let's hope the inside looks better than the out.' Sadie said, reached into her purse and chucked a few coins in the homeless man's plastic tub before heading up the steps for the door.

A bell jingled as she pushed through it.

Unfortunately, the interior wasn't much better. The tables looked to be clean and the waitress that greeted them had a pleasant smile on her face, but the room had a foul smell lingering around it. Half of the booths looked dark and glum from where the bulbs had blown in the lights that hung above. The leather on the seats had huge cracks running through them and there weren't as many people working the floor as there should be.

'Table for three, is it?' the waitress, Izzy, as the pin on her uniform had stated, pointed over to a booth next to the window, that still had a bulb working above it.

They headed over, Peter slid in, and Sadie sat next to him. Emily sat across from them. They took a moment to consider the menu and thought the safest option would be to each order a cheeseburger, fries and a milkshake.

'I'll apologise now, Emily,' Sadie began, picking the salt-shaker from the condiments tray and rubbing the grease between her thumb and index finger, 'if the milkshakes aren't as tasty as I had promised you. This used to be such a nice diner.'

Emily smiled and looked out the window, watching as cars and trucks on the motorway raced past. A movement to her left caught her eye, and she saw the homeless man who was sleeping outside had stood. He kicked over an empty beer can and headed for the entrance. She presumed perhaps he needed to use the toilet.

'I wonder what happened to this place?' Peter asked over the sound of the bell above the entrance door jingling.

'You see it all the time,' Sadie began with a look of sorrow. 'Restaurants are bought out by competing companies who expect to turn things around, instead they just mess everything up and then claim bankruptcy in a year.'

'Well, we won't be stopping here on our way back when driving you home,' Peter commented and then looked at Emily. 'Emily, are you alright?'

Emily didn't answer. She was too busy observing the homeless man, who was now stood at the front, next to the counter where a couple of truckers sat sipping coffee. The homeless man was tall, standing over six feet. He looked around the restaurant, his head moving left to right slowly, as if he was drunk... or still sleeping. His droopy eyes fixed on Emily, and he began dragging his feet as he started for her table.

'Emily?' Peter asked, turning to see what she was looking at. He watched as the approaching man reached for something off a nearby table and, as he clutched it tightly, Peter could see it was a steak knife. 'Gran, watch out!'

Sadie turned just in time to see the man swipe at her, the blade narrowly missing her throat as she jerked backwards on the cushioned seat. Seeing her opportunity, Sadie pushed at the man's side, and he stumbled away, but kept his balance. Sadie stood from the booth and backed away as Peter slid out and kicked at the man's feet as he went to charge for his gran. This time he lost his balance and landed on the floor with a loud thud, dropping the knife and watching as it slid away.

'Emily, come on!' Peter shouted, ushering her out of the booth as he kept his arms spread out, making sure Sadie was behind him. Emily quickly slid from the booth and joined his side as the homeless man got to his feet and reached for the knife.

'Look at his eyes,' Peter said.

'He... he looks asleep!' Emily confirmed.

'Just like yours had last night,' Peter sighed. 'They're open, but he isn't aware of what he's doing. He's being controlled!'

'Dylan, what are you doing?' Izzy, the waitress, asked as she left the kitchen.

'Hey, put the knife down!' a man called from one table who'd witnessed him fall to the floor. 'You don't need to rob these people; I'll buy you some food, man.'

The homeless man began heading for Sadie again, his sleepy eyes only fixed on her.

'This is Mary Anne,' Sadie called, backing further away, with Peter in front. 'She's the one controlling him.'

Izzy shot them a look of confusion and ran back into the kitchen, calling for help.

Peter pulled a wooden chair from under one of the unoccupied tables and held it out in front of him, jabbing it forward as if the man was a dangerous lion at a circus act. 'Get out... Come on!' he ordered Sadie and Emily. Emily held onto Sadie's hand, helping her through the main door and then down the steps.

The man was swinging the knife out in front of him, trying to catch Peter with it, but he couldn't get close enough. Peter backed down the steps and reached into his pocket for his car keys, pressed the button to unlock the doors and once he saw Emily and Sadie were safely in the car, he tossed the chair at the man and raced for the driver's door. The chair connected with the sleeping man's shoulder, causing him to grunt and misjudge the last step. Peter dived behind the wheel and watched as the man tumbled down the steps, then got to his knees. Peter quickly inserted the key into the ignition and started the car, backed out of the parking space and took off with a screech from the tyres.

Emily turned in her seat and peered through the back window. She could see the man was trying to follow behind them, dropping further and further away as the car sped down the slip road, readying to join the motorway. When it became clear he would not catch up, the homeless man turned to his left, saw a truck approaching, and stepped out in front of it.

'NO!' Emily gasped and closed her eyes as the truck's horn blared.

'What did you see?' Sadie asked. 'He won't catch us now, not on foot.'

'He's dead...' Emily murmured, turned back around and slumped down in the seat, resting her head in the palms of her hands.

'What? How do you know-'

'He's just stepped...' Emily stopped and shook her head. 'Mary Anne made him step out in front of a truck.'

The steering wheel made a squeaking sound under Peter's tight grip. 'That bitch!' he hissed as his eyes glazed over. 'She's never going to stop hurting innocent people, is she?'

'No, she isn't,' Sadie confirmed, pinching the bridge of her nose. 'As if that poor man didn't have enough to worry about.'

'Yeah.' Peter nodded.

'She had that man trying to kill me... Which means she knows exactly what we're up to. She knows we're heading back to Hollow Tower to trap her again.'

'No...' Peter shook his head, cleared his throat, and turned to face her. 'Not just trap her, Gran. This time we stop her for good, permanently. We need to find that doll and rid ourselves of that evil bitch once and for all, so she can't hurt anyone else.'

Emily stayed quiet; picturing how different her life would

be today if she forced Chloe to stay away from the fifth floor. She, Chloe, Hannah, and Amy would all be in the office right now, probably laughing or rolling their eyes as they spoke to an annoying customer.

After joining the motorway and traveling some miles, Peter asked, 'Are you okay back there, Emily?'

'No, Peter,' Emily answered, and wiped away the tears rolling down her cheeks. 'I'm really not okay.'

Chapter 17

'Let's wash up first,' Peter began as he parked the car at the side of Hollow Tower, in the residents' only private car park. 'I'll find some torches and grab us a snack, just something to tide us over until we deal with her. I don't know about you, but after we're done, I'm heading out for a bloody good beer.'

'I think we've been through enough today,' Sadie said, unclipping her seatbelt and opening the car door. 'Why don't we leave it till the morning? It'll be getting dark soon and we'll need as much light as we can to find the doll that belonged to Paige. God knows where Mary Anne might have hidden it.'

'No.' Peter argued, staring straight ahead, watching a Magpie that had landed on the roof of the car opposite before taking flight again.

'Excuse me?' Sadie asked, turning to face her grandson head on.

'I said *no*, Gran. We can't trust what Mary Anne might do next. An innocent man has already died today. Who's going to be next? You? Emily? Everyone that lives in this building?'

Sadie shot Emily a quick glance and looked back at Peter. She knew he was right. The quicker the evil spirit was dealt with, the better. 'You're right, Pete. Dark or not, let's do it today and put this thing to bed. I know I wouldn't have slept much, anyway; I can already feel her presence here.'

Peter nodded. 'I'm not sure if I'll ever sleep right again. Knowing entities like Mary Anne exist only makes me wonder what else is out there.'

'That alright with you, Emily?' Sadie asked. 'If we jump straight in and get this done now?'

Emily nodded. 'The quicker the better, right? I don't want to be climbing into Peter's bed again.'

'What's that?' Sadie asked, raising an eyebrow and smirking.

'I'll explain later, Gran,' Peter said, and they stepped from the car.

Sadie clutched onto her overnight bag, tilted her head up to the darkened windows on the top floor and thought, *I knew one day I'd be back here to deal with you!*

'Ready, Gran?' Peter asked and after Sadie nodded, the three of them headed into the building and crossed the lobby. Before they could reach the lift, Harry's apartment door flung open, and he and Margaret stepped out. 'Sadie!' Harry called and embraced the elderly lady in a hug. 'You wasn't going to say hello?'

Sadie hugged him back, then moved over and quickly hugged Margaret. 'Of course I was, but I was going to do it after I'd dealt with the trouble on the top floor. We can't waste any more time. She's... she's already hurt someone today trying to get to me.'

Harry and Margaret both looked at each other, then back to Sadie. 'Whose life has she claimed now?' Harry asked.

'A homeless chap's,' Sadie nodded with a look of guilt etched onto her face, as if it was her fault the tall homeless man had died earlier. 'She got into his head while he was sleeping, controlled him the way she does.'

There was a loud sigh from both Harry and Margaret.

'I would have had a knife in my throat if it wasn't for Emily seeing him approaching our table.'

'Jesus,' Harry muttered, running a hand across his stubbly cheeks. 'That poor guy... But I'm glad to see you're all okay, though.'

'I wouldn't say we're *okay*, Harry. But we made it here in one piece. I guess that's something.'

'We've been waiting for you to arrive all day,' Harry said, resting a hand across the top of Margaret's shoulders. 'Margaret and I have been, excuse my French, scared shitless to leave our apartment in case she got a hold of us. We're so glad you're here.'

'No, you've been safe today. She's been busy elsewhere.'

'I'm going to pop upstairs,' Peter said as he pressed the button for the lift. 'I've been bursting for a pee for the last hour and could do with splashing some water onto my face.'

Emily was ready to say she'll head up with him, go to her own apartment to freshen up, but then Harry rested a hand on her shoulder and Peter was already standing in the narrow lift with the doors closing behind him.

'How are you holding up with all of this, Emily?' Harry asked.

What should she tell him, that she was overrun with guilt for releasing Mary Anne from the spell that had kept her bound for so long? Or that ever since hearing about an evil spirit possessing the fifth floor, she's been waiting for a film crew to jump out from behind a wall and explain she's been the victim of a prank? 'I just... I just want... *need* this to-to end...' was all Emily managed before she broke out crying. Margaret moved over and pulled her in, hugging her tight.

'You've all had a long drive,' Harry said, pushing his apartment door open and stepping inside. 'Come on, I'll stick the kettle on, and you can relax for a bit.'

Margaret walked Emily inside, still holding her close, and sat her down on the sofa. 'I guess a cup of tea wouldn't hurt,' Sadie said, stepping into the landlord's apartment. 'I'm sure Peter will be happy to have a quick rest.'

'I'm sorry,' Emily said, wiping the tears from her eyes. 'It just all caught up with me... everything that has happened and-'

'Hey, don't apologise, love,' Harry said, and Margaret nodded, offering her a warm smile. 'It's a lot for anyone to process, never mind a young woman such as yourself.'

Harry left for the kitchen and returned a few minutes later with a tray of steaming mugs and a plate of biscuits. Each of them took a mug and began chatting. After Emily finished her tea, she slumped back on the comfortable sofa and listened as Sadie and Harry spoke about the past. Margaret would occasionally write a question on the magnetic drawing board she kept at the side of her chair, and Sadie would laugh and answer. With the three friends occupied with catching up, and the lack of sleep she's had, Emily soon nodded off to sleep.

She dreamt she was sitting on her sofa in her own apartment. The terror over the last few days had never happened and Mary Anne didn't exist. Chloe hadn't been tortured and then murdered. The fifth floor in Hollow Tower wasn't closed off and instead, it had families living happily up there. Life was good, and Emily was thoroughly enjoying it.

After hearing a light knock on her door, Emily muted the TV, stood and headed over to answer it. Jasmine Dale was standing on her welcome mat, asking to borrow some sugar and promising that she'd replace it when she headed to the shop. 'Of course,' Emily smiled and invited the woman in. Jasmine followed her kind neighbour inside and waited for Emily to fetch the sugar from the cupboard. 'Oh, wow...' Jasmine gasped, taking in the recently decorated living room as they passed for the kitchen. 'You've got this place looking lovely.'

Emily tipped some sugar out of the bag, half filling a cup and then turned to face her neighbour. 'Thanks, I did most of the painting myself-' she stopped, discovering she was alone in the kitchen. Placing the cup on the counter, she took a few steps forward, seeing if the woman had wandered off to inspect the rest of the apartment. 'Jasmine?' Emily called and was answered with a low chuckle. Though she was unable to pinpoint where the sound was coming from, as if the sound was coming from within the walls. 'Jasmine?' Emily tried again, but this time, she was ignored. 'Jasmine, are you still here?'

Running water was heard from the bathroom down the hall, so Emily headed down and stood outside the door. 'Jasmine, are you in there?'

'NO!' a deep voice called back, followed by a mighty bang as the door rattled furiously against the frame. 'NO. NO. NO.'

'Jas... Jasmine?' Emily called again and the rattling door abruptly stopped, then the handle turned and the door slowly creaked open. Emily waited, expecting to see her neighbour step out and offer an explanation. But the bathroom was empty.

Emily stepped into the room, her bare feet standing on the cold tiles as she checked behind the door, finding no one hiding behind it, she headed over to the taps to switch the water off. Looking up at the mirror, she saw a tall man standing in the corner, watching her. She spun around, expecting the stranger to be gone and that her mind had been playing tricks on her. Only the stranger was still there, his dirty clothes filled with many holes hung off his thin body. He had blood gushing from multiple wounds and his leg was broken, the bone was poking out of his skin and then through the denim of his tatty jeans. The lower part of his face drooped to one side, and his jaw looked as though it had been crushed. 'You... you did this to me,' the homeless looking man slurred. 'You did this!'

Emily shrieked and ran back out to the corridor, heading for the front door, but stopped at the sight of her friend Chloe, who was standing blocking the exit. 'Chloe, what are you doing here–' Emily began, studying her friend's naked body with numerous slices across her skin. 'What the hell has happened to you?'

'You!' Chloe replied in an aggressive tone, her eyes burning into Emily's as she stepped towards her. '*You* did this to me... You!'

'No,' Emily said, backing away and sprinting down the corridor for her bedroom. She pushed the door open and dived under the duvet sheet on her bed. 'I need to wake up. I need to wake–' she stopped when she heard the bedroom door open and then close. She could feel someone standing there, sense them watching her. Whether it was the strange man from the bathroom, or her work colleague, it didn't matter. She didn't want to remove the duvet and face the horror. Didn't want to know who – or rather, what – was in her room. But she had to, she knew that.

Slowly removing the duvet from her face and peering out, she saw an old lady standing in the corner. Unlike the man and Chloe, the old lady looked small and fragile. She had no broken bones sticking out of her skin and no slices visible on her body. Instead, her skin looked extremely pale, almost transparent, the pupils of her eyes were dull, cloudy and lifeless. 'Who are...' Emily swallowed, licked her lips and started again. 'Who are you?'

'Ada,' the old lady in the corner answered, smiling with thin, cracked lips. 'My name is Ada, and you did this to me!'

'I... I don't know who you are!' Emily whispered back. In her dream, Emily had never met the old woman before.

Ada stepped forward, her movement quick and stealth like, not the stride you'd expect from an elderly person. 'Yes, dear... you did this to me.'

'I-I'm sorry, but I didn't!'

Ada jolted forward as a thick slice opened across her throat and blood pooled out, her sweet face changing into something that resembled a demon as her hands reached out, squeezing around Emily's throat. The old woman's skinny fingers dug into her skin.

'No, Ada!' Emily screamed and jerked upright, seeing Harry, Margaret and Sadie all turn and look at her.

'Did you say Ada?' Sadie asked with a look of concern on her face.

'What?' Emily looked around the room, noticing she was still on her landlord's sofa.

'You just called out for Ada,' Sadie shifted in her seat. 'Were you dreaming of her?'

'I... Yes, I did,' Emily confirmed. 'But something was... *off* with her. She looked-' Emily didn't finish, she didn't want to frighten Sadie any further.

Though it didn't matter, Sadie already had a look of fear on her face as she immediately stood from the other end of the sofa and said, 'I should have checked in with her earlier, informed her we've arrived safely. I know she's probably worried sick right now.'

'Here, Sadie, you can use my phone,' Harry said, reaching into his pocket and pulling out his mobile.

'Thanks.' Sadie took the phone and walked off towards the kitchen, rapidly tapping a number onto the screen.

Emily noticed an untouched mug of tea resting on the coffee table in the middle of hers and Sadie's cups. 'Is that Peter's tea?'

'Yep. Well, it *was*,' Harry answered. 'He's probably having a nap up there. No doubt needed to rest his head for a little, especially after such a long drive.'

'How long have I been asleep for?'

'Only half an hour. I'm guessing you must have needed it too.'

'Peter hasn't come down yet?' Emily asked, standing and fixing her hair over her shoulder.

'No,' Harry wheezed. 'We thought it would be best to leave him to nap. All that driving on an empty stomach can't be good for him. Poor man is probably exhausted.'

'I'll go up and check on him,' Emily said and headed for the door.

'Come on, pick up the phone, Ada!' she heard Sadie plead, and a terrible feeling ran through her.

When the doors opened and Emily stepped out of the old lift on the fourth floor, she walked towards Peter's apartment and noticed the door was ajar. She pushed it open further and stepped into his darkened corridor, finding a small table had been knocked over and the lamp that was resting on top was now broken and lying in pieces on the floor.

'Peter?' Emily called, heading further into his apartment and flicking on a light when she reached the living room. She screamed, holding a hand up to her mouth after finding Peter bloodied and tied to a chair. Then she narrowed her eyes and was filled with anger when noticing who the man was standing next to him.

Chapter 18

'Josh!' Emily roared, heading further into the living room. It was obvious from the mess - the broken coffee table and the shelf that had been knocked off the wall - that the two men had fought and, unfortunately, Josh had gotten the upper hand. 'What the hell are you doing here?'

'I've... I've come for you, m-my love...' Josh, Emily's ex-boyfriend, slurred as he held onto a bottle of whiskey and fought to stand upright.

'What?' Emily asked.

'You mess... messaged me,' Josh said, stepping from behind the sofa and standing in front of Emily. The reek of alcohol escaping him caused her to wince at the smell. 'You sent me a message, ex-explaining how much you had missed me and... and that... that you needed my help...'

'He was waiting outside in the hallway when I came up,' Peter confirmed, blood leaving a cut on his lip and travelling down his chin, then onto the front of his t-shirt. 'He asked me what apartment yours was and then turned aggressive when I refused to tell him-'

'You... shut up!' Josh shouted, turned to face him and shot him an angry look. 'You don't-don't deserve to s-speak to her.'

Peter continued, 'Then he told me he was here to save you, that your *neighbour* has been abusive, treating you wrong. That I've been keeping you against your will?'

'What?' Emily asked again, unable to make sense of what she was hearing.

'Don't y-you worry now. I'm he-here, love. I've come... like you asked... I've done what you wanted me t-to. We can be together... again.'

'Are you crazy?' Emily shouted and Josh's face dropped, as if he'd received a slap.

'But you mess-messaged me!'

'No, I never, Josh. You're clearly drunk and confused.'

Josh pulled his mobile from his pocket, dropped it to the floor, bent to pick it back up, and then tapped at the screen before turning it around for Emily to see. Emily studied the number at the top of the message, shocked that it did, in fact, belong to herself, then read the message.

Josh, this is Emily.

I know it's been a while since we last spoke, but I miss and need you!

I've been wanting to call, but my neighbour, a man named Peter Dunn, is keeping me against my will. He hurts me and is extremely abusive. I'm scared of him. If he knows I've sent this message, he will kill me.

Please, you must help me!

I'm on the fourth floor at Hollow Tower, Hollow Street, facing the park entrance.

DO NOT REPLY TO THIS MESSAGE, FOR MY OWN SAFETY.

I love you.

Emily

'I came as... as soon as I could, I've been waiting outside all d-day for you to get home!'

'Emily?' Peter said, waiting for her to look at him. 'Is it true, has the message been sent from your mobile?'

Emily nodded and Peter knew exactly what has happened. He shook his head and sighed, 'Bloody Mary Anne!'

'Her name is Em-Emily!' Josh slurred.

'I don't remember sending it, Peter. Apart from a nap on Harry and Margaret's sofa just before, I've been awake all day!' Emily said. 'I stayed awake last night too, keeping myself awake so you could sleep, remember?'

Peter shook his head. 'I remember. But you slept earlier!'

Josh moved his glare back to Peter, then studied Emily with a confused look on his face. 'What is... is going on... here?'

Emily stared at Peter, waiting for him to explain.

'In the car, when we hit all that traffic because of the accident on the motorway,' Peter flinched from the pain in his lip. 'I saw you on your mobile, tapping at the screen.'

'You did?' Emily asked.

'Yes. You answered me sounding a little dazed, like you've just woken up from a nap. I'm guessing you must have sent it then.'

'I'm here, now,' Josh smiled, taking a sip of the whiskey he had taken from Peter's kitchen. 'I kn-know I messed up, b-but we can be together again. We can make things right between-'

'What the hell is all this?' Harry asked as he stepped in and dropped the bucket and lighter fluid on the floor that Peter and Emily left in his living room last night. Margaret and Sadie came in behind him and gasped.

'Oh, Peter!' Sadie called and began over to help him.

'Woah, woah,' Josh yelled and raced over to stand behind

Peter taped to the chair. He grabbed a kitchen knife he had stored on a shelf behind him and held it to Peter's throat. 'S-stay... stay back...'

'Who are you?' Sadie asked, her eyes darting from her hurt grandson, then back to the drunken stranger.

'I'm here to... help... Emily. To save her from... from him!' Josh slurred again, nudging Peter on the side of the head with the knife handle.

Emily wanted the ground to open up and swallow her whole as the three of them all looked her way. Josh was an embarrassment, a drunken one that she thought she'd escaped from. Keeping her address private, changing her mobile number and even using a different name on social media were the lengths she'd taken to keep him out of her life. And now here he was, hurting her new friend that had agreed to help her clear the miss she had made.

'Emily, do you know this man?' Sadie asked with a judgemental look in her eyes.

Emily nodded her head and released a loud sigh. 'Unfortunately, Sadie, I used to... Once, I guess.'

'What do you want from us?' Harry asked, stepping closer. 'There is no need for violence, son.'

'I'm here... to save her from this abuse... abuse... from this man,' Josh answered.

'If we let you take Emily with you, will you leave?' Harry asked, and Emily shot him a look. He gave her a subtle wink and looked back at the drunken man with the knife.

'I'll leave with you, Josh,' Emily swiftly nodded. 'Just you and me, like you want.'

Josh grinned and blinked, the alcohol in his system causing him to stumble slightly.

'We could go-go for a drink?' Josh asked.

'Sounds good!' Emily smiled.

'No... none of you...try to stop... try to...'

'None of us will stop you.' Harry confirmed. 'Just put the knife down and leave, now!'

Emily held out her hand and Josh walked away from Peter. He placed the knife down next to the fish tank, but kept hold of the bottle of whiskey.

'You absolute idiot!' Emily hissed once there was distance between him and the knife. Josh's smile suddenly dropped.

Emily pushed him away as Harry tackled him to the floor. Josh attempted to use the whiskey bottle as a weapon and tried to whack Harry on the head, but missed and dropped it. Harry was wheezing more heavily than normal now, but kept Josh in a tight grip. Margaret noticed the strong duct tape resting on the broken coffee table that he'd used to restrict Peter, so she grabbed it and tied Josh's wrists and ankles together.

'I'll call the police,' Emily said and pulled out her mobile.

'Wait,' Peter yelled, and everyone turned to look at him. He nodded towards the window, where outside the sky was growing darker by the minute. 'Dealing with the police will only slow us down more. We must fight Mary Anne first, make sure she's gone, then we can deal with him later.'

'Em... Emily... h-help me,' Josh begged. 'I came h-here for you. I tried to-to help you!'

'Shut up, Josh!' Emily roared. 'You drunken waste of space.'

Harry used the kitchen knife to cut Peter out of the tape. Peter stood, swung his arms around to loosen them up and raced for the kitchen, opening and closing drawers. He returned a moment later holding two torches, switching both on and off to check they worked. 'I only have the two, so we'll have to share.'

'It won't help much, but I can use the torch on my mobile,' Emily said, pulling it out of her jeans pocket.

'Alright,' Sadie began. 'Let's be quick up there-' she stopped as the framed picture of her and Peter picnicking in the park flew across the room and struck her on the side of the head, instantly drawing blood from her temple.

'What the...' Josh mumbled after witnessing it.

'Gran!' Peter cried, raced over and caught her before she tumbled over.

'I'm fine... She's trying to stop us,' Sadie confirmed.

'Then we have to move quick,' Peter said. 'We'll search each room together, in and out. In and-' Before Peter could finish, the fish tank exploded, sending water, glass and fish spilling onto the floor.

'Jesus!' Harry cried. 'Those poor fish. I'll grab a pan and we can try to save some of them.'

'Leave it!' Peter ordered. 'She's trying to slow us down and we mustn't let her.'

'He's right!' Sadie called, holding a finger up to her cut, applying pressure. She headed for the door, holding onto Peter's arm for support. 'Come on, we have to do this now.'

They left his living room and began down the corridor as every bulb in the apartment exploded one after the other, sending shards of glass raining down above them. Peter switched on the two torches, then held one out for someone to grab. It was Margaret who reached for it, and she aimed it in front of her and Harry to share. Peter and Sadie shared his one and Emily followed close behind with her iPhone torch activated, leaving Josh in the living room, calling her name and begging to be set free.

They left his front door and began down the corridor.

'Don't race off up the stairs without us,' Harry wheezed. 'Give us old ones a chance to keep up, yeah?'

'I hope you're not involving me as one of *the oldies*?' Sadie joked, but no one laughed. They'd all seen for themselves or have heard stories of what Mary Anne was capable of, so it was normal for each of them to be feeling petrified of what might happen.

One minute later, they were all standing outside of the door that opened onto the fifth floor. Harry and Sadie paused for a few seconds to catch their breaths as Margaret rubbed at the top of her husband's back.

'In and out,' Peter said again, breathing heavily from the thought of what he's about to do. 'Let's be quick in there.'

Harry studied the broken lock on the door and sighed. Emily noticed the annoyance on his face but chose not to say anything. Other than apologise again, what more could she have said?

'Is everyone ready for this?' Peter asked and Sadie and Emily both replied with "NO!"

Margaret shook her head as Harry murmured, 'As I'll ever be.'

'Good,' Peter nodded. 'Let's go.'

Chapter 19

Peter opened the door and each of them entered the corridor, waiting for Sadie to give the go ahead. Sadie reached into her overnight bag and pulled out an old-looking book that was leather-bound and extremely thick. 'Peter,' she called. 'Give me some light.'

Peter shone the torch onto the book as Sadie flicked through the pages, stopping halfway through and nodding. 'This is the spell.' She put her hand back into the bag again and pulled out a green pendant that had spots of dark red in the middle.

'What's that?' Emily asked, intrigued.

Sadie smiled and slipped the pendant necklace over her head. 'This pendant protects me as I'm reading the passage,' she held it up for Emily to see. 'The spots in the middle are mine, my mother's blood and my grandmother's blood, plus their mother's before them. Generations of powerful witches stop me from coming to harm from anything supernatural as I'm performing the spell.'

'So, you're like... untouchable in there?' Emily asked.

'Unfortunately, no,' Sadie sighed. 'I can still be hurt. Mary Anne can use one of you to cause me harm, either by controlling you, picking debris up and sending it my way, or by causing the walls to crumble. We just have to keep her away from me as long as we can while I finish the reading.'

'Let's get this-' Harry began, but stopped as every door on the corridor flew open and slammed shut again. 'Fuck, here we go!'

Each of them shivered as the temperature in the corridor suddenly dropped and Mary Anne appeared at the far end of it. She stood tall with her claw-like fingers dangling at her sides. Her eyes were wide and glowing brightly in the dark as she screamed, 'You!' Then she pointed a bony finger at Sadie as she darted down the corridor, aiming for her.

Sadie began reading the passage before Mary Anne had the chance to reach her. Mary Anne stopped on the spot, hissing and crying as smoke began at her feet. She pointed a finger at Peter and a moment later he was flung against the wall, crashing into it before landing on the floor, breaking Sadie's spell. Emily, thinking quickly, rushed to Sadie's side and shone her torchlight on the book. Sadie began reading again and Mary Anne hissed some more, staring at her with an evil glare. 'I'm going to butcher you like I did your friend!' she shrieked and sunk into the floor, disappearing.

'Come on,' Harry called. He was carrying the metal bucket with the lighter fluid and matches in and helped Peter up from the floor. 'Let's get in that apartment and search for this bloody doll while we still can.'

'Where is she?' Emily asked, looking all around. 'I just watched her disappear into the bloody ground!'

'She can do a lot more than that,' Sadie confirmed. 'But she'll be back. The spell I'm casting works immediately, tears her up from the inside, causing agonising pain. If she doesn't escape quick, she'll be stuck on the spot until I finish and force her soul back into the doll.'

'Then we burn the damn thing once the moment comes available!' Emily nodded.

Harry, with Margaret clutching onto his arm, opened Mary Anne's old apartment door, and they all entered, shining their torches around.

* * *

Below, lying in the dark room on the sofa with his wrists and ankles restricted, Josh could hear the commotion from the floor above. He fought to free himself but couldn't. The tape was wrapped around so tightly that all he was achieving was pain and discomfort.

'Fuck!' he roared around the quiet room, becoming agitated. 'You bastards!'

Confusion ran through his mind as he thought about what had taken place earlier. Why did Emily say she hadn't asked for his help, then blame it on a woman called Mary Anne? How did that picture frame fly across the room like that? Why are Emily and a bunch of strangers heading upstairs to fight with this Mary Anne person?

He thought about the words of the man who he had attacked, about calling the police when they were finished doing whatever it is they're doing upstairs, and an uncomfortable feeling turned his stomach.

I can't go to prison.

He knew a man like himself wouldn't survive in a place like that. Sure, he was a dick. He'd happily admit that. He was fully aware of how much of a selfish prick he had been throughout the years too, but he wasn't bad enough for prison. That place is for the *real* criminals. What he had done by attacking that man was in the name of love. Love for Emily.

'I did it for you, Emily!' Josh sobbed quietly. 'I only did this for you.'

'Yes...' a woman's quiet voice called from the dark and Josh shrieked. 'She'll know that soon.'

'Who's there?' Josh shouted. The room was in complete darkness and now had an icy feel to it. 'Who are you?'

'That doesn't matter right now, Josh.' The woman answered. 'Names aren't important... only freedom is.'

'You're... you're that Mary person, aren't you?' Josh asked, listening to the sound of broken glass crunch under foot.

'I know you came here for Emily,' the woman said, moving closer until her lips were next to Josh's ear and he could feel the danger she brought with her. 'She might not know it right now, but she will one day.'

'W-what do y-you want?' Josh stuttered.

'I want your help.'

Josh scoffed and buried his face into a cushion. Being tied up and with the thought of the police coming to arrest him, he had began to sober up.

'Why should I help you?'

'Because I can help you in return!' the woman said, gripping him under the chin and holding his face up. He winced from how deadly cold her fingers were. 'I have the power to make Emily love you again. You and she can be one, the way you both used to be.'

'Yeah, right!' Josh murmured.

The woman brought her face closer and squeezed her hand

tighter. Even in the pitch black, Josh could see the glow of her icy blue eyes as she stared into his. He knew then this Mary Anne woman wasn't normal. That she wasn't human.

'You can't control who Emily loves-' he broke off as his mind was taken elsewhere.

'Just concentrate...' Mary Anne's voiced faded as Josh day-dreamed.

What he was seeing felt incredibly real, like a memory. Only he knew it wasn't, because Josh had no memories of owning a huge house in a suburban neighbourhood. In the scene that the woman was showing him, he and Emily were smiling in a well-kept garden as two young children ran about, laughing and playing on the grass. Emily was sitting in a deck chair, holding a glass of wine as the sun beamed down on her face. Josh could see her watching him with pure love and admiration in her eyes as he was stood at a barbecue, turning over a couple of burgers and holding a beer. The scene was a cliché, straight out of a happy family TV advert that was probably selling something like *life insurance*, but Josh didn't care. What this woman was showing him was happiness. It was utter perfection.

For Josh, it has been far too long since he had felt genuine pleasure, and he couldn't help but smile. Then the woman holding his face took away her cold fingers and Josh almost sobbed as he was brought back to reality, back to the dark living room of the stranger who he had attacked earlier. The same stranger that would be calling the police and having him locked up and sent to prison with the "real criminals".

'Well?' the woman asked.

'Please, show me more,' Josh begged, desperate to feel that happiness again. 'Just one more minute, please!'

'No,' Mary Anne denied. 'Nothing is free!'

'What do you need me to do?' he asked in a low whisper as a tear rolled down his cheek. He needed to be back there, in that daydream, back in that simulation, or whatever this strange woman wanted to call it. He just had to be back, to feel the contentment again, to experience more of that joy. He'll do anything for it.

'You know the woman who came in earlier,' she began, her breath so close to Josh's face he could smell the death it carried. 'I want you to kill her for me!'

Josh swallowed. He would do anything to have that life with Emily, but could he commit murder?

'I... you... you want me to ki-kill her?' Josh struggled, praying he didn't hear her right.

'Yes!' the thing next to him confirmed.

'I don't know if I... There must be something else I could do! Please?'

'You can refuse,' Mary Anne snickered. 'You can stay here and wait for the police to turn up and you can lose Emily forever.'

Before he could say anything, Mary Anne held onto his face again and he was forced to look into her glowing blue eyes. Only this time, Josh wasn't in a happy place, smiling. He tried to pull himself away, not liking what she was showing him, but he couldn't. Her grip was like a vice. In this simulation, the woman didn't need to create fake scenarios, instead she simply showed Josh sitting in his local pub - *Ray's Bar.* She showed him the barmaid, Kayla, looking at him with disgust and hatred. Mary Anne fast-forwarded a few hours - past the scene that showed Josh gulping down beer after beer while sitting alone–then she showed him stumbling home, passing happy couples as they held hands and laughed together. The next scene showed him sitting on the old, torn sofa that belonged to his father, watching whatever rubbish was on TV before falling asleep. Then doing the same thing all over again the very next day. His life was boring, miserable, and repetitive.

I don't want that! Josh thought.

'Please... stop!' Josh cried, trying to shake away her hands. 'Please... I-I don't want to see that.'

'No!' Mary Anne sneered, and Josh was thrown into another scene. Like the one earlier, in the well-kept garden with the sun shining and the children playing, Josh was standing next to the barbecue as another man worked the grill. Though not just any man, it was the guy from upstairs, the one who Josh had attacked. He was laughing and sipping the beer Josh should have been drinking.

This future Josh had experienced before belonged to the guy upstairs, not him and Emily. It was the *stranger's* and Emily's!

'No, please...' Josh cried. 'Please, stop!'

Mary Anne held on a little longer, fast forwarding the day until she showed him Peter and Emily sitting on the sofa, snuggling and watching a movie. Then she finally removed her grip from his face and Josh dropped his head onto the sofa cushion, crying.

'So, now you see, you can refuse and go back to your life,' Mary Anne chuckled. 'Or you can do as I ask and-'

'I'll do it!' Josh agreed at once. 'I'll do whatever you need... Just-just give me what you showed me first... Give me *that* life. Me with Emily, please!'

Mary Anne lifted a finger and, using her demon claw-like nails, swiped at the duct tape restraining Josh's wrists, then moved further down and freed his ankles.

'Dead, do you hear me?' the woman asked, burning her eyes into Josh's.

Josh stood from the sofa and took a moment to answer while

he rubbed at his wrists, feeling the stickiness on his skin.

Mary Anne lunged for him, pushing him back. With her face pressed up against his, she screamed, 'Dead, I want her dead! Did you hear me?'

Josh nodded obediently and stuttered, 'Yes... Yes, I-I heard y-you...'

'Do not fail me...' Mary Anne barked as the glow from her eyes dimmed. 'You'll pay the price if you do.'

Josh reached for his mobile from his pocket and activated the torch, shining it around Peter's dark apartment. Mary Anne was nowhere to be seen.

* * *

Sadie was still reading from the book, her words coming out fast and clear.

'Where is she?' asked Harry, his back up against the wall as he shone the torch around. 'Does anyone see her?'

'I don't see her!' Peter said. 'Emily?'

'No,' Emily answered, using the little light that her iPhone offered. 'I can't see-'

'Emily?' Peter shouted, unable to take his torch from the book that Sadie was reading from.

'Who has left?' Emily asked.

'No one, we're all still here. Why?'

'I thought I heard the door... out in the corridor.'

'Margaret and I are still here,' Harry confirmed, his chest wheezing. 'Obviously so is Sadie.'

'Gran has almost finished,' Peter cheered. 'Just a little further and Mary Anne will be bound again–'

SMACK!

'Peter!' Sadie cried, followed by the sound of a second *SMACK* and then a thud.

'Sadie?' Harry called 'Peter, are you both okay?'

Harry shone his torch over to where Sadie was standing and yelled, 'You stupid bastard!'

Emily turned away from the wall she was searching and, with Harry's torch lighting up that area of the room, she saw Josh standing over Peter and Sadie with a table leg in his hand.

Chapter 20

'No!' Emily gasped, seeing Peter on the floor, holding a hand to the back of his head. She ran over and dropped next to Sadie, calling her name, but the elderly woman wouldn't wake. 'Please, wake up. Come on, please!'

Harry rushed over, yelling, 'Do you know what you've done?'

'I did it for us, Em–' was all Josh managed to say before Harry grabbed the collar of his shirt and pushed him away. Josh tried to swing out the table leg he had gotten from Peter's broken coffee table, but Harry dodged it and Josh missed. The two men hit the ground next to the door for the balcony and fought. Harry climbed on top of Josh and began punching him repeatedly. Josh tried to protect his face and push him off, but Harry was like a rabid dog.

What he had mentioned earlier about there being no need for violence seemed to have gone right out of the window.

Margaret was at their side, attempting to pull her husband away and break up the fight.

Josh reached for Harry's throat and dug his thumb in, causing the landlord to wheeze and splutter. Margaret grabbed the torch from the floor that Harry had dropped and bashed it across Josh's face, busting his nose open. Eventually, Josh stopped fighting and went limp. His hand fell away from Harry's throat. Margaret helped her husband to stand, pulled him away and sat him on the floor, rubbing the top of his back as he struggled to catch his breath.

'Gran?' Peter called, sounding dazed. 'Gran, are you okay?'

'She's breathing,' Emily confirmed, feeling for a pulse. 'But she's unconscious.'

'Fuck. Now what are we going to do?'

'Do you think you could read the passage?' Emily asked.

'No, I wouldn't even know what part to start from–'

Sadie's thick, leather-bound book slid across the dusty floor, over to the corner of the room. Peter reached for his torch and shone the light in its direction, only to find Mary Anne standing behind the book, grinning with a sadistic look on her face. 'Old Sadie can't help you now!' she cackled.

'We're fucked!' Peter shrieked and Mary Anne nodded in agreement, showing a wide smile of rotting crooked teeth.

'We need to find that doll,' Emily whispered. 'Unless you can read that passage, destroying the doll is our only hope!' She shone her phone torch towards Harry and Margaret and vaguely made out Margaret's subtle nod that she had heard her.

'Come on!' Emily began and started for the opposite corner of the room, running along the wall with her iPhone torch shining on the floor and along the skirting boards, searching for any gaps or misplaced pieces of wood.

Margaret put a hand on Harry's shoulder, and he nodded he was okay. Then she snuck off and headed into the kitchen, searching the empty cupboards and under the sink. Coming up empty-handed, she stepped back into the living room and was stopped by Mary Anne, standing on top of the dark stain on the floor. Her evil glare dropped to the stain as a smirk grew on her lips before looking back up to face Margaret. 'What can I have you cut off next?' she mocked, her eyes looking at her ears and then around her face. 'Didn't you learn your lesson last time?'

Margaret backed away, heading further into the kitchen until her back hit the sink.

Seeing Mary Anne was distracted, Peter tapped a hand against Sadie's cheek, trying to wake her. But it was no good. The old woman was clearly out cold.

He quietly moved down the corridor to search the bathroom, removing the panel from the bathtub, finding only dead flies and cobwebs behind it. He lifted the lid off the toilet tank, seeing nothing inside before crouching to search the floor, hoping to find a loose floorboard.

Nothing.

A loud crashing sound was heard from the kitchen.

'Harry, Margaret, are you okay?' Peter called, turning down the corridor and making his way back.

'Help her!' Harry wheezed loudly before breaking into a coughing fit. 'Peter, please, help Margaret!'

The torch Margaret was using came rolling across the living room floor. Emily reached for it before heading into the kitchen to find Margaret being controlled by Mary Anne like a puppet, tossed about on top of the work services. Margaret screamed as she was bashed left to right against cupboards, and then lifted in the air before being dropped to the floor, causing the air to be knocked out of her. Mary Anne stood laughing as the woman on the floor groaned in pain.

'Leave her alone!' Emily shouted and Mary Anne spun her head in her direction.

'Killing your friend wasn't enough for you?' she smirked. 'Now you want to be a hero?'

Harry, with his back still against the living room wall, shouted, 'You leave us alone, you evil bitch!'

But Mary Anne didn't show him attention, she just kept her glare on Emily and sneered, 'I've broken much stronger people than you!'

Emily backed away before sprinting out of the living room and into the corridor, bumping into Peter. Mary Anne raised her claw like finger and an invisible force lifted Emily into the air before throwing her against the wall. She cried out and fell to the floor, clutching her arm as Peter knelt at her side. 'Keep searching!' Emily ordered him.

Mary Anne appeared behind them and chuckled. 'You're never going to find it. The lot of you are going to die trying!'

With her blue eyes focused on Peter's, she raised another finger, but instead of throwing him to the side, she curled her hand into a tight fist. Peter felt as though his throat was being crushed, like there was a heavy foot standing on his windpipe and he dropped to his knees.

Emily got to her feet and saw Peter gasping for air. She backed further down the corridor, shouting, 'You're as ugly as that doll I found!'

Mary Anne scrunched her face in anger, released her hold on Peter's throat and raised a hand, lifting Emily high before sending her crashing into a door, causing it to break open.

Peter sucked at air before crawling into the living room to find Margaret helping Sadie to sit up.

'Thank God!' he wheezed in a low tone, rubbing at his throat. 'She's going to kill Emily; you have to start again, Gran!'

Emily lifted her head from the dusty ground and coughed. Even though she was aching in pain, she couldn't help but smile when she heard the low, raspy voice that belonged to Sadie as she began reading the passage again. Mary Anne turned away, roared, and then vanished from the room.

Emily stood, readying to leave the bedroom and head back to join the rest, to keep the fight going, but then stopped as her eyes caught sight of the wallpaper.

She's been here before.

Only she knew that wasn't plausible, because when she and Chloe first came up here, they only saw the living room and the doorway that led to the connecting kitchen. They never stepped foot in any of the bedrooms, so how can she possibly recognise the wallpaper?

Then a thought came to her, and she gasped. The colour of the wallpaper was forest green, and it had patterns of small, red roses dotted about. It was the same wallpaper she had found stuck under her fingernails the morning she had woken with filthy feet and pyjamas covered in dust. Emily has been here before, just not awake!

With the sounds of Sadie reading, the demonic roars from Mary Anne and the cries of pain from Harry, Margaret and Peter as the maleficent spirit tortured them to keep her freedom, Emily knew she had to act quickly. She shone the torch around the room, searching but not seeing any signs of a hiding space.

Slow down! She told herself, realising she was rushing. *Just slow down and search properly.*

Emily started again, moving the torchlight slowly across the wall until she came to a spot where the wallpaper had been torn away, just above an electrical outlet. She raced over, dropped to her knees, and held onto the plastic case secured to the wall. She yanked at it, and it fell off right away. Emily wanted to scream with joy when she saw what was in the gap. The doll!

The electrical outlet had no wires, as if the case was only a decoy. The doll was nestled in the back, behind a few pieces of broken wood and crumbled plaster.

Emily reached for it, stood and ran down the corridor for the living room. The bucket with the lighter fluid and box of matches that Harry had carried in was to her left, in the corner of the room. Sadie looked pale and weak, but she was still chanting loudly, and it was sending Mary Anne insane. Mary Anne roared and shrieked as she lashed her arms out, trying to slice Sadie with her claws, but she couldn't reach. Sadie's pendent was working, keeping the invisible barrier around her, protecting her. Emily knew the spell must have been working, because Mary Anne could no longer move her legs. The wooden floorboards were rising and dropping as she fought and cried out, but still the bottoms of her soles didn't leave them, as if her feet had been nailed down.

Josh, looking dazed and confused, stood with his face all bloody from receiving a beating off Harry. 'I'm not losing my future with Emily!' he yelled, reached for the table leg off the floor and tossed it in Sadie's direction. Luckily, it missed Sadie by a couple of inches, however, it interrupted her reading for just a moment. But then she continued, proving it wasn't long enough for Mary Anne to escape the hold.

'You failed me!' Mary Anne screamed, held out her arms and sent Josh flying backwards. Before he could crash into it, the door that led to the balcony swung open and Josh toppled over the railing, falling five floors to the ground below.

'Josh!' Emily cried, gaining Mary Anne's attention. She spun her head, preparing to unleash some cruel words, but then noticed Emily was clutching onto her daughter's doll - Paige's doll. Her eyes widened and the aggressive expression on her face softened, leaving the appearance of a hurt old lady.

'Emily,' she began in an innocent voice that was hard to believe belonged to her. 'Don't destroy that, please! It's all I have.'

Sadie continued reading as Emily headed for the bucket. She tipped out the can of lighter fluid and box of matches onto the floor, then dropped the doll inside.

'I didn't want to hurt anyone,' Mary Anne whimpered. 'I was forced to do those things.'

'Don't listen to her, Emily,' Peter said as he stood at the side of his grandmother, holding the torchlight to the book pages. Mary Anne hissed at him and then went back to staring at Emily.

'What about Chloe?' Emily asked, squirting the fluid onto the doll until it was drenched, and the can was empty.

Mary Anne's innocent expression cracked as she knew it was the end. Her lips spread across her entire face, and she hissed, 'She was a whore who had it coming!'

Emily shook her head, sparked a match and said, 'Wrong answer, bitch!' Then dropped the match into the bucket, engulfing the doll in flames. Mary Anne cried out in pain as a ball of fire appeared at her feet before snaking up her body. Just before the fire could claim her head, the evil spirit turned to Sadie, smiled and sneered, 'I'll say hi to Ada for you!'

Then she was gone, and the room fell silent, the only noise coming from the wind as it blew in through the open balcony door. Sadie collapsed to the ground and Peter dropped to his knees next to her. Margaret crawled over and sat at her side, embracing her in a hug and rubbing the top of her back.

'I knew something was wrong when Ada didn't answer her phone earlier...' Sadie sobbed from the floor, looking exhausted as tears ran down her cheeks. 'I just knew something was wrong.'

'I'm sorry, Sadie,' Harry sighed, shuffling himself along the floor to place an arm around Sadie's shoulders.

'She'll be with Helen,' Sadie nodded, wiping the tears from her cheeks. 'She'll be with her Helen now.'

'I'm sorry, Sadie,' Emily said, wishing she could turn back time and drag Chloe by the scruff of her neck away from the door. 'I'm sorry... *everyone*!'

'You did it,' Peter smiled and nodded at the bucket of fire. 'You got rid of her!'

A floorboard behind Emily creaked and everyone shrieked, waiting for Mary Anne to return and cause more havoc. Peter raised his torch to the doorway, and they all watched as the ghost of a man walked past. He was dressed in a white shirt that was untucked from his trousers and had paint stains all along his sleeves. He stopped to look in at them all, meeting the eyes of each person in the room before nodding and walking off.

'That was Richard Belton,' Harry began. 'The painter who jumped from the window. The man who went insane, claiming he saw Mary Anne everywhere he went.'

Next came a woman with a young boy standing in front of her. The woman had freckled cheeks and long ginger hair, dressed in a white floral print dress. The boy had blonde hair, also freckled cheeks, and was dressed in blue pyjamas with patterns of small sailboats. The ginger woman smiled, and the little boy waved. Right behind them was a man dressed in and a grey suit, salmon coloured shirt and a yellow tie. He rested his hand on the woman's shoulder and nodded before they continued. 'That was the Hickling family,' Harry confirmed. 'Kevin, the schoolteacher, his wife Maxine and their boy Joseph. I'm guessing they couldn't move on... couldn't find peace until Mary Anne was... *defeated*?'

For the next few minutes, as the doll in the bucket continued to burn, Sadie and the residents of Hollow Tower all waited and received a wave, a nod or a simple smile as Harry explained who they were and what awful act Mary Anne had forced them to commit.

As the fire in the bucket died, and the last of the victims who had once lived on the fifth floor was gone, Peter rubbed at his face and said, 'I don't know about anyone else, but I would kill for a beer!'

Chapter 21

ONE MONTH LATER

Emily knocks on Peter's door holding a travel mug that was white in colour and decorated with pictures of open books and coffee cups.

'Morning, love,' Sadie called, after opening the door. Sadie had moved back into Hollow Tower after she travelled home to Sheffield and found Ada dead at the foot of the stairs. 'Oh, no, Peter won't like that you've opened your gift early!' she laughed, nodding to the travel mug.

'I just couldn't wait any longer,' Emily replied, stepping into the apartment. 'I couldn't take my eyes off it last night. It was calling my name, begging me to open it–'

'Are you serious?' Peter asked, rushing over. 'It isn't your birthday until tomorrow, Emily! You should have waited...'

'I told you,' Sadie smirked and headed back into the living room.

'I'm sorry. I couldn't wait any longer. It's a very thoughtful gift.'

'Hmm,' Peter frowned and pulled on his coat. 'Well, seeing as you're bringing it along, you can try your first cup of coffee in it when we get to the Hollow Grill.'

As an early birthday treat, Peter had offered to take Emily for breakfast in the Hollow Grill and Restaurant, as she's back in the office tomorrow morning, and then will head to her parents for dinner.

'Gran, are you sure you don't want to join us for breakfast?' Peter shouted into the living room.

'Don't worry about me, love,' Sadie declined the offer. 'One of my morning TV shows will be starting shortly. I'll see to myself.'

Emily and Peter left the apartment, headed down the corridor, and pressed the button to call the lift. When the old doors rattled open, they stepped into the confined area and Emily hit the button for the ground floor. She eyed the space for the missing fifth floor button and turned to face Peter. 'Has Harry mentioned anything about refurbishing the top floor yet?'

'I passed him the other day in the lobby,' Peter answered, 'overhearing him and Margaret discussing it... Well, it was more like *arguing* over it. Harry wanted to start work soon, get a team in and receive some quotes on what it will cost to renovate the entire floor, but Margaret wouldn't have it.'

'Oh?' Emily chuckled.

'Yeah, I heard her tell him they should forget about it, leave it as it is. You know, after all what had happened up there throughout the years, all the deaths, I can't say I blame her.'

'I know I wouldn't want to rent an apartment knowing it once belonged to an evil spirit that tormented the residents for years.'

'I agree,' Peter said as the lift came to a stop, jolted a little and the doors opened onto the lobby. They left Hollow Tower and crossed the road into the park.

They walked slowly, taking in the morning sunshine, nodding good morning at passing dog walkers. As they reached the middle of the park, they both turned back to face the building. 'I still can't believe we beat that bitch!' Peter laughed, looking up at the fifth-floor windows.

'I know,' Emily agreed, studying the balcony that Josh fell from. 'I can't believe Josh survived the fall!'

'Right?' Peter chuckled. 'When Mary Anne pushed him, I thought he would be dead for sure. If it weren't for those bushes breaking his fall...'

'Yep. As if he's only suffering with a broken leg and two splintered arms. What a lucky bastard.'

'Has he... has he tried contacting you?' Josh asked.

'No. I visited him in the hospital a couple of weeks ago, just to check in on him, to see how badly he was hurt. You know what he said to me?'

'Go on...' Peter ushered her.

'He asked me to leave!' Emily laughed, brushing away a piece of rogue hair that had fallen in front of her eyes. 'He asked *me* to leave *him* alone!'

Peter shook his head and smirked.

'Yep,' Emily smiled. 'All it took for him to get over me was coming face to face with Mary Anne and being pushed over a fifth-floor balcony. He said I was strange. No, weird. That I was *weird* for being friends with you all and playing about with evil spirits.'

Peter laughed loudly. 'That cheeky git!'

'If I'm being honest, I think he's waiting to be arrested, you know, for attacking you and Sadie that night.'

'I figured he'd been through enough. Besides, I already threatened him that if he didn't leave you alone, I would go to the police to tell them everything. How he broke into my apartment, kidnapped me, beat me, hurt Sadie.'

'You threatened him?' Emily asked, unable to hide the smile growing on her lips. 'When was this?'

'Yeah. It was a few days after it happened,' Peter confirmed, looking to the ground and kicking away a stone. 'I told him he was lucky to have escaped with his life, so enjoy what he can of it without you. I asked him what he told the police had happened, and he said he'd told them he'd fallen from the balcony after stumbling into the building drunk.'

'Well, it seemed to have worked. Josh hasn't messaged or rang me once. I'm finally free of him.'

'That cheap travel mug wasn't really your birthday present; it was keeping that dick away,' Peter joked, and Emily laughed.

Before turning away from Hollow Tower, Emily studied each of the grimy windows on the top floor and shrieked when she thought she saw a grey-haired figure dart away.

'What is it?' Peter asked, noticing how she had become rigid. 'Emily, what did you see?'

Emily stared at the same window, then moved to the ones either side of it, but she saw nothing else. 'I thought... I thought I saw... I don't know what I saw. It was probably nothing, I guess.'

'It's normal to feel that way,' Peter explained, nodded hello at a dog walker and then added, 'What she put you through, the things you were made to see. The way she... the way she murdered your friend, I don't think you'll ever completely forget about Mary Anne.'

'Yeah,' Emily swallowed. 'She's always going to be on my mind, that's for sure.'

'How have you been holding up?' Peter asked with a concern look on his face. 'Have you been sleeping okay of a night?'

'Same as always,' Emily lied, but she knew Peter could tell.

The truth was, Emily would wake almost every night in a cold sweat and scream out. Mary Anne occupied her dreams, reminding her of the evil she had done, not just to Chloe, but to whoever had crossed her path. Emily didn't want Peter knowing this because she didn't want him to worry about her. She guessed he too, along with Sadie, Harry and Margaret, will always have Mary Anne on their minds, or roaming their nightmares. They might be able to forget her for a few days, maybe even a week, but she'll be that horrible memory they can't seem to shake.

'Are you sure you're feeling okay?' Peter asked, running a hand up her arm.

'Yeah,' Emily replied, clutching hold of his hand. 'I'm starving, let's go eat.'

They turned to walk through the rest of the park. Peter went to take back his hand, but Emily kept hold of it, keeping it in her grip. Peter shot her a nervous grin.

Reaching the door of the restaurant, Peter grabbed the handle and opened it for Emily to enter first. 'I can't believe you've lived across from this place for a whole two months without trying the breakfast. They do the best pancakes around.'

'I blame you for that,' Emily joked. 'You should have asked me on a date sooner.'

'This... this is a-a date?' Peter stuttered.

'I'd like it to be...'

'Me too!' Peter replied, and they found a table at the back, close to a window where they could people watch.

A WORD FROM THE AUTHOR

Hello, you lovely reader. I just wanted to say a huge thank you for choosing to read my book. I hoped you thoroughly enjoyed it and will come back for more from me in the future.

If you did enjoy the story, please consider leaving a review on Amazon and Goodreads. I appreciate every single review I get, and it also lets me know if I'm doing a good enough job :)

Until next time, take care and thanks again.

D. R. CLARK

Printed in Great Britain
by Amazon

39685528R00091